DRAGON WINTER

Published by Mundania Press
Also by Don Callander

Pyromancer
Aquamancer
Geomancer
Aeromancer
Marbleheart
The Reluctant Knight

Dragon Companion
Dragon Rescue
Dragon Tempest
Dragon Winter

Warlock's Bar & Grill
Warlock's All & Sundry

Teddybear, Teddybear

Cruise of the CSS Pocahontas

Star Warrior

DRAGON WINTER

DON CALLANDER

Production by Celeritas Unlimited LLC
Printed in the United States of America
10   9   8   7   6   5   4   3   2   1

DEDICATION

To *all* Redheads and especially my two favorites: my wife of more than 36 years, Margaret Millikan Nash Walker Callander; and my best friend, Bruce Knight Cleworth. Both no longer are redheaded—due to age not vanity—but both are still great friends.

--- Don Callander (an aging blond), 2007

Chapter One
Storm Clouds Gather

A racing white blizzard blasted across the high passes and over lower peaks of the Snow Mountains, flung itself across Gugglerun Ridge and full upon Murdan's Overhall.

The thermometer nailed outside the Lord Historian's bedroom window almost shattered as it showed *minus fifteen degrees* of bitter cold.

Outside the stables piles of fresh horse droppings steamed like miniature volcanoes but froze to the icy cobbles before a shivering stable boy could run out to shovel it up and away!

Proud young Chanticleer, the Overhall Cock-of-the-Walk, gargled his usually clear salute to the hidden sunrise, shook his red and blue tailfeathers, and pranced back into the nice, warm coop to console his two dozen brown hens and warn them to stay inside as much as possible.

Two little girls—one the daughter of an Innkeeper; the other a Princess and the daughter of a Princess and grand-daughter of a King—slipped and skidded on the new snow in the outer bailey, lugging a bucket of wheat and corn and barley and a bit of stale bread crumbs to the hens in the coop, all the while giggling and shrieking with pretended fear of falling.

On the steep steps from Middle Bailey to Outer Bailey, red-cheeked sons of Overhall guardsmen, and a sprinkling of apprentices from kitchen and armory and buttery, showed Gregor Clemsson how to bellyflop down the hill on their tummies, screaming with glee.

Gregor's younger brother Tommy at first held back out of sensible caution—and then flung himself down the slope headfirst, shouting his shrill defiance of the danger.

If Gregor could do it, *he* would do it better! And faster and louder, too.

Sir Thomas Whitehead of Hidden Canyon Achievement, Knight Royal, Librarian to the Historian of Overhall as well as to the King of Carolna, carefully laid aside the bulky book he'd been carefully re-binding—*Ancient and Arcane Lore & Essential Charms*, one of his employer's most ancient and most precious tomes—and went to the window of Lord Murdan's study to watch the boys sliding by with breakneck speed.

"It's going to be a real killer of a blizzard," Tom said to Murdan.

"What are you, a weather prognosticator?" grunted his master.

Murdan was writing in a ledger with a long grey goose quill and didn't look up as he spoke.

"I'm an Iowa boy and I know a blizzard when I see one coming," Tom insisted. "Even the pigeons are staying in their cote and the corbies under the eaves, too. I bet the cows in the byre are standing as close together as maids watching a Fall Sessions Parade just to keep warm."

Murdan looked up, at that, and grinned broadly at his friend and employee. He rose and glanced through the window, and then reached for his warmest winter cloak.

"In which case we're obliged to go try the slope, ourselves, Librarian. Make sure nobody gets hurt, you understand."

"Of course! Clem made me a pair of cross-country skis. I wonder how I could do. Haven't skied in years and years."

Murdan shooed him out the door, saying, "We'll do it young Tommy's way—on our stomachs! Ledgers and bankbooks can wait until the snow *really* shuts us indoors."

Princess Alix Amanda Trusslo-Whitehead of Hidden Canyon pricked her ring finger with her embroidery needle and swore a very unladylike oath.

"It *is* getting too dark in here," observed Mistress Grumble. "I shall order more candles, Princess."

Manda, as she preferred to be called, sucked her stabbed finger and reached for a bandage from her sewing basket.

"No, *no!* This is not a morning for sewing, Grumble dear. I'd better see what Gale is doing. Even *I* get lost here at Overhall, comes darkness!"

"The child, bless her heart, is never in danger at Overhall. I saw her playing with Brenda, from Sprend. The girl from the Babbling Bass, you know?"

"Oh, yes!—happy little pixie, Brenda! They've become bosom buddies, staunch playmates, as little girls often do at their age."

"And the Innkeeper's family is *most* respectable. Sensible—if they *do* always seem to smell of—well, you know! But if my poor old bones tell me true, Manda, this storm is going to be ferocious! Listen to that wind! I think I'd better make sure all windows and doors are shut tight! Will you excuse me?"

"Of course! And I'll just make sure of the girls. Goodness! The snow on the level is already ankle deep!"

"And just beginning! I hope Captain Graham's men are clearing the ways. *And* the drawbridge! Snow gets very heavy, you know."

"Why not just lift the drawbridge?" asked a guard corporal—who also happened to be Graham's middle son. "The snow would just—slide off, Daddy."

"My boy! What if someone should come seeking shelter from the storm? To find Overhall Gate shut tight! Lord Murdan would spout steam from his ears and fire from his eyes."

"I'll take care of it, Dad!"

And the young man turned away to fetch off-duty guardsmen who were throwing snowballs at each other in front of the barracks. "*Hey!* Brooms at the ready! Hartfeel! Fetch a sack or two of rock salt! We're to clear the draw and plow the Gateway. Everybody look lively, now!"

Tom bent to help the Historian to his feet at the bottom of the slope between Middle and Outer Bailey. The two men laughed like little boys and brushed snow from their clothes.

"Here's a beautiful snow-maiden," Murdan cried on seeing Manda, Gay, and Brenda. "No! Three of 'em! Good morrow, ladies!"

"Mama says it is going to snow for a long time," Princess Gale Thomasdotter bubbled, throwing her arms about her father's waist and waving to the puffing Historian at the same time. "Can I slide, too?"

"You *may*— if you don't mind climbing the hill to Middle Bailey," her father said. "I'll go with you! Coming, Mother?"

"Mayhap we should go inside. It's turning cold! Well, just once or twice, I agree. It's been a long, long while since I saw or felt or tasted or slid on snow," Manda said as they climbed. "Mornie says it snows like this up to their cabin several times a winter. Never snows much, ever, in Hidden Lake Canyon, however."

"All the more reason to enjoy it while it's here for us," her husband said.

They all ate lunch—fried chicken and hot baking powder biscuits—in front of a snapping fire of seasoned oak logs in the castle kitchen. It was bright, clean, and, most important, warm as toast.

"You'd think all this stonework would be good insulation," Tom was saying to Murdan. "I suppose once the walls get cold it takes a magic spell to warm them up?"

"Never thought of it, to tell you the truth! Mostly they're warm enough in summer, however." Murdan considered the matter. "Not a bad idea, however, I'll bespeak Arcolas on it. He's from the North and ought to know about such things."

"How much will it snow, Daddy?" Gay asked around a chicken leg she was chewing.

"Don't talk when your mouth is full," her mother said. "Swallow first!"

"Yes, Mama!"

"As to how much, I surely don't know. Maybe Arcolas can answer that. He has some knowledge of weather, I believe. I haven't seen Master Arcolas in a week or more," Manda said, carefully swallowing a bit of biscuit and raspberry jam first.

"He probably foresaw this storm and took a vacation down south. He was intending to spend some time helping young Findles in Aquanelle," the Lord Historian put in.

"He could have warned us," Tom muttered.

"What good, that? The only thing you can do about storms is endure 'em. Hunker down and tolerate!"

"Well, if you will excuse us, wife and daughter, Murdan and I intend to insulate ourselves with a ton and a half of scrambled papers on the silver-works in Lexor. Formal supper, tonight, Murdan?"

"Yes, it just makes sense. All my people together in one room provide plenty of body heat. And it keeps the servants warm running back and forth to the kitchen!"

They all stopped talking as they heard a booming from far off, through the muffling snowfall.

"Someone's knocking at the gate," cried Murdan angrily. "Who closed the gate?"

"*I* ordered them swung-to," Captain Graham admitted. "It seemed best. The north wind was shaking the jambs out of the stone. And it helped keep the Lower Bailey clear of new snow!"

"Well, go bring whoever it is in to thaw. Noontide or midnight, Over-hall welcomes *all* strangers in a storm!"

CHAPTER TWO
Dragons at the Gate

When his second son Corporal Greysolon—Grey, for short—under Graham's order tried to force the main gate to swing open, the huge leaves proved stuck fast.

"*Here!* Lend a shoulder or two!" the young man wailed in frustration. "Barney! Donad! *Papa!*"

All four put shoulders to banging the left-hand leaf until it slowly began to swing outward. Someone was helping by scraping the packed snow from the outside.

The guardsmen stared in wonder at the swirling haze of ice crystals, black wings a-beating, and a great cloud of acrid pink seam that filled the gateway.

And they laughed in relief.

"Sweep the draw clear for us, Retruance Constable, please! There may be others lost in the blizzard behind you!"

The great head, eyes, and saber-like teeth of the Dragon in the snow emerged from the broil, shook itself and roared above the wind.

"Another comes, fellows! Brother Furbetrance is trodding on me tail!"

Sure enough, in a fast minute *two* Dragons were clear of the snow and steam shaking themselves like two huge dogs, and grinning in satisfaction.

"Here's a poor, lost traveler almost frozen solid, too," Retruance called, very serious all at once. "Woodsman Clematis Herronsson! Found him buried to the topknot just below High Pass. We feared the worst! That he was fairly frozen solid, you must know, but he's breathing a bit yet and our inner fires have kept him alive."

Corporal Grey sent Barney running ahead to announce the arrivals and warn of an urgent medical emergency. Retruance gently carried the half-frozen man to the open door of Foretower and surrendered him to Murdan and Tom.

"You didn't fly?" the Historian barked, helping to bear the burden to the nearest fireplace in the Dining Hall.

"Visibility down to zero," the older Constable huffed. "We landed in Pass in the first place because we couldn't see ten yards ahead!"

"Came the rest of the way by dead reckoning, we did!" Furbetrance said over his brother's shoulder. "Is he—is he—*well?*"

"Not really very well," Tom answered, working swiftly to doff his best friend's ice-stiff clothing. "Frostbitten, I'm almost sure."

"Arcolas!" the Historian bellowed.

"Not back yet," Tom reminded him. " Mayhap Mistress Grumble would best know…"

"*Fetch Grumble!*" Murdan bawled. "And heat a caldron of water!"

"*No* boiling water!" Overhall's housekeeper said when she arrived, running. "Bathe his feet and hands and ears in snow first. Poor laddy! The cure's more painful than the malady, I know."

Naked on the warm hearth, Clem shook like a leaf but endured the melted slush without complaint.

"When you're done thawing me out, Mistress, I think I broke a leg, too. Have a care! Lower left leg; at the ankle."

"I sees it and I knows a bit about setting bones, too, so don't get upset, Woodsman. Soon as the inner cold warms a mite, I'll see to the leg. Someone feed him a stiff brandy!"

"He'll be a-right?" Manda, just arrived, spoke in a trembling whisper, "He'll not…lose his leg?"

"Not if *I* can help it, Princess! And that's all can be done for a short while. Drink this warming brandy, Woodsman, and try to sleep a while. Setting an ankle is not a pleasant…"

You have nothing to kill the pain?" Tom asked.

"I've given him a bit of Numbing Praise, and he will sleep, now."

"*Numbing Praise?* Laudanum, I suspect," Tom murmured. "I am often surprised by the folk remedies you use, Grumble!"

"There are no bad medicines," the housekeeper sniffed. "Only stupid doctors!"

She ordered a cot brought from a ground-floor bedroom. They carefully lifted the stricken Woodsman onto the cot, for the hearth was hard and almost hot enough to burn bare skin.

Clem muttered a few slurred words but didn't waken.

Well," Murdan sighed, turning away and addressing the Dragons at the window. "I think we avoided great tragedy this time, thanks to you Constables."

"Pleasure, to be sure!" Retruance said, blushing a deep green. "We sort of—well—*stumbled* on poor Clem in a snowdrift. By accident! I imagine he can blame me for the broken ankle."

"Nobody with him?" Manda inquired.

"No, Princess! We searched very carefully and Clem was able to tell us he was alone. He knew Mornie and his sons were here, of course."

"Is it still snowing?" Tom asked a snow-covered Graham, just returning from inspecting his on-duty soldiers and civilians striving to clear the courtyards and stairways of snow.

"Not a bit less, as yet! And blowing stronger! Sir?" He turned to Murdan as Tom helped him shed his heavy coat.

"Yes, my friend. You want to give your men a rest?"

"We can't go on all night. It's gotten much colder."

"Where is that dratted fool Magi when I need him?" the Historian growled angrily. "Well—stand them down. Tell Cook to give them a big, hot meal. Everybody is still working. We'll just have to wait it out, *then* dig it out."

"Good decision!" Tom agreed. "We'd all get some sleep."

"Get up as soon as the snow slows or stops, then." Murdan nodded. "So be it! Everybody eat something and go to bed. Nothing more we can do."

"If somebody else comes knocking at the gate?" Manda asked her husband as they climbed to their apartment halfway up Middletower.

"Not much we can do ourselves, I fear. Dragons will stand by. They need less sleep than us. Time to crawl into bed under several of those down comforters your stepmother sent us."

"We did bring them along, didn't we? Oh, yes, I remember now."

They entered their suite, greeted by their Overhall nursemaid, the Sprend girl named Brenda. While Manda went to check on their daughter, asleep in her cozy nursery, Tom advised Brenda to take a comforter and a pillow and bed down on a couch near the fire.

"You'd not make Main Gate in this weather," he told her. "Let alone Sprend."

"I'll wake-and-stoke, then," sighed the lass. "Be there enough firewood?"

"I *think* so. I had the box filled this morning; it seems a week ago, now. If you run short of billets, wake me. Don't be alarmed if a Dragon comes to the window. But I suspect you know Retruance well, by now?"

"Like a great green puppy, Sir Librarian! And thank you for asking!"

"He may come to our bed chamber window, actually. Ah, well—to bed! Snow is fun until you have to shovel it."

Furbetrance Constable entwined his forty-five feet of blue-tiled head, torso and tail—not to forget black wings—around the inner pillars of Great Hall, contributing his body warmth to a sleeping staff, mostly pages, chambermaids and waiters bundled in wool blankets and embroidered curtains, huddled close together and as near the two dining hall fires as possible.

The kitchen staff, below stairs, had snuggled close around the huge ovens in the Bakery. Off-duty guardsmen wrapped themselves in their fur winter cloaks and jackets, close to their barracks' fires.

Although Tom had personally worked on it for years, the hot air system he'd designed for Overhall Castle was far from completed—especially in the underground cellars, dungeons and warehouses and at the tops of the three towers, where rising heated air fought year-round with the prevailing winds.

Mornie, Clem's wife, sat wearily erect almost within the Dining Hall fireplace, watching her sleeping husband. She had wrapped their two sons in rugs and sent them off to sleep with friends elsewhere in the Hall, against their protests.

"He's breathing most easily now," she whispered to the Dragon. "No fever or shaking. No great pain!"

"Bunk down beside him, then! I'll watch until these folks wake and start breakfast. We'll all soon need hot food, I'm sure."

"No doubt about that, Furbetrance! And Clem'll argue when I try to keep him in bed a bit longer. I know this boy so very well!"

The Dragon examined the trapper closely once again as Mornie crept under the covers beside him.

"He'll walk in pain for a few days. But I judge all will be well with him—and you, dear Mornie. Sleep easy!"

The young lady smiled wanly and released a deep sigh of comfort and reassurance from the words of the great beast.

And dropped into deep slumber.

Tom woke at morning Change of Guard in the courtyard below his bedroom window. The one-handed clock high on the south face of After-tower snapped, groaned, then tolled six times.

He listened to the reassuring crunch of boots in the darkness, the clacking of pikestaffs and the rattle of longbows. Beyond those sounds he could hear someone whistling cheerily in the kitchen.

"Hey?" said the far rank of eiderdown pillows.

"Stay warm and cozy. I want to go check on Clem."

"*Ummm,*" the pillow agreed.

The Librarian glanced into the nursery. Gay slept, still and deep and rosy-warm, smiling slightly. As he headed for the door, Maid Brenda stirred and raised her head.

"Breakfast soon. Let 'em sleep, Brenda! Go get yourself some griddle cakes and the latest news. Manda'll want t' know what's going on."

"Yessir! Is it still snowing?"

"Don't know! Windows iced over solid."

He found Clem and Mornie, wrapped in each other's arms, with Mornie asleep but the Woodsman wide awake.

"She sat up half the night, a-watching me, I swear," Clem whispered. "Needs the sleep."

"The boys?"

"*Uh*—over there somewhere."

"They're okay then. How about you, Clematis, old icicle?"

"Feet tingle like crazy! I haven't tried to stand yet."

"Mother Grumble thawed you out and wrapped your toes," said Mornie without opening her eyes. "G'morning Tom! Is it still snowing?"

"I'll go look," Tom promised. "Do you feel like walking a bit, Clem?"

"Try! All I can do."

Furbetrance opened one blue eye and nodded to the two friends as they staggered across the floor to the front door, which now stood ajar.

"Stay here and keep things snug, Furbie." The Librarian grinned. "We're just going to see the weather."

"Snow stopped an hour ago," Furbetrance called softly after them. "Turned really cold, though!"

"We're snowbound, for sure," Clem said, forcing his painful feet to carry him across the foyer to the main Foretower door. "Musta dropped twenty inches—or more."

"Much more! Lend a shoulder here…"

More snow had been wrapped around the tower base and piled up six feet high to block the entrance. It took six men to shovel and push the door wide enough to allow passage.

"We've some shoveling yet to do, I guess." Clem sighed. "I hear somebody digging, over to the Guard barracks."

"Not a job for the frostbit. Let the boys move the snow; clear the ways. Let's go get some breakfast. I guess the kitchen's open and humming. And nice and warm! Smell that bread!"

Clem sat to ease his throbbing feet and a waiter brought them steaming cups of tea and slabs of warm, fragrant white bread with butter and strawberry jam.

"Bacon? Ham?" asked a serving boy. "How do you want your eggs, sirs?"

"As if I was particular! Bring a little everything, Cyrus. My gut thinks I cut me throat." Clem both laughed and groaned.

"I'll collect your boys, then," Tom told him. "Be right back."

"Hold off a moment, Tom! I—I—just remembered…"

Clem had been on a last late sales trip to Wall on the northwest coast, selling bundled furs and enjoying a bachelor's holiday. The crowds at the inns and pubs of Wall were a tough bunch, a mixture of trappers and deep-sea sailors.

Mornie and the boys were visiting Overhall instead, planning to return to their cabin in the deep forest of Lakeland before winter set in.

Clem recalled something he'd heard while on the sales trip. "A ship's officer I know—a friend of my sea-going brother Cus—sought me out one night. His ship had been northwest into the Boring Sea that summer for seals and such, he said. While there they heard talk of Northmen preparing to invade Carolna come *spring!*"

"We drove those wilderness men back once before—but that was over in the Northeast and years ago." Tom's brow furrowed. "Called themselves Rellings, as I recall."

"Maybe the same folks? Maybe a new gang. I need to tell of it to the Lord Historian as soon as I can climb to his place up above. Warn the King as soon as this storm blows over! It might be important."

"No doubt of it!" Tom stood. "Let me speak to Murdan right now, while you greet your lads. If I know Murdan, he'll come down to you!"

CHAPTER THREE
Rumors and Plans

Murdan dropped heavily into his chair at the head of the Long Table whose highly polished surface reflected the worried, tired, and anxious faces of a dozen friends, family and retainers.

Some were missing. Murdan's son-in-law Ffallmar and his Rosemary were snowbound at Ffallmar Farm, thirty miles to the east.

Also missing was Arcolas the Physician. The Historian valued the little man not so much for his knowledge of healing medicines, but for his wide knowledge of Magicians, Wizards, Witches and Scholars.

Murdan looked up when Manda, Tom and Clem entered, nodding apologetically. The Woodsman was using crutches, slowed by his frostbitten feet.

"We will begin, then," was all the Historian said. "Princess? You are the ranking member…"

"Not in your own house!"

Manda seated herself on Murdan's right.

Murdan nodded, accepting her decision not to preside. "Tom? Sit here on my left."

He then went on, "I wish Arcolas was here. I've sent off reliable pigeons but…no word and we will not wait further.

"We have received most distressing news from a sailor Master Clem bespoke at Wall just seven days ago. Repeat it for us all, Woodsman, and then we'll discuss it."

Clem carefully retold the story told him by his sailor friend, saying his name to be Fogler.

"I don't recall that name," Graham said. "Do you, Lord Historian?"

"It's a common one and I've asked Tom to look it up, hoping perhaps his name would appear somewhere in our records. Tom?"

"No mention—except as a *family* name. Most of the Foglers were and are Blue seafarers."

"I have known him for twenty years," Clem insisted. "He has honest repute."

"Good enough for me, then," the Historian decided. "Further questions?"

Tom looked up at the faces of Retruance and his brother in the tall Conference Room windows.

"You guys know this family? And how about the wilder-men he mentioned, out in that direction?"

Retruance shook his head slowly and Arbitrance shrugged his massive shoulders, adding:

"I would ask Byron Boldface, who lived a long time in Hintoo, which is south of that area."

"Good advice. Where is the good Byron, then?"

"Still on the middle west coastland of Isthmusi with his people," Manda put in. "We've visited them three or four times. They are such nice people and their climate is almost *too* perfect! No snow nor ice!"

"Except atop the mountains," Retruance murmured, but then louder he added, "There's your old friend Hoarling Ice Dragon, Murdan. He might know what's going on up there. Or could find out."

"Good idea! Hoarling is not the most genial Dragon around, however."

"Let us talk to him, however," Tom, who was Retruance's Companion, suggested. "A very good idea, I would say."

Several other suggestions were put forth, but the council only accepted the first two.

"Tom and Retruance to find the Ice Dragon. See what he knows—or can find out," Murdan decided, "and I'll send Clem on Furbetrance to Isthmusi, to talk to Byron."

"Clem is not yet fully recovered," Princess Amanda objected.

"A tropical vacation should do him a world of good. And Mornie and their boys can go with him."

"Good! But you must send *me* with *my* husband!"

"I cannot object, dear Princess. But the *child?*"

"She goes, too. Part of her education, I say!"

Nobody, not even Murdan, objected.

"*I* will go to the King," he announced. "And prepare for possible invasion."

"I must say, sir, such a winter journey is not for a little girl of seven. Terrible things could happen, m'lord!"

This came in a whisper from Brenda of Sprend who had squeezed into the Conference Room gallery unnoticed.

"Then I appoint *you* to go along, missy," chuckled Murdan. "Care for the little princess and free her parents from distractions!"

"Oh, all is right then, Lord Historian!" cried the maid. "When do we start—and what should I wear?"

Manda took Brenda by the hand and led her down the Grand Staircase. By the time they reached her apartment, they had planned a sensible wardrobe with accessories.

"The Master? Won't he need things like weapons and such?" the maiden asked.

"That's *his* business, I think. Actually, I don't ever recall Tom carrying weapons. He usually depends on his brain."

"I've heard he is not—*uh*—like unto others. He's said to be a…"

"Human? It's so! My husband saved my father's kingdom more than once with his Human ways and means, even if they are different than yours or mine."

"Oh, *I* have no powers at all," Brenda protested, dragging a canvas rucksack from a closet.

"All people and all creatures have powers. We'll see if yours include packing for a journey northward in winter. Let me see…where did I have our winter gear stored?"

"We're wearing it." Her husband, just arrived, laughed. "I think we'll need some more wool flannel underwear, Manda."

"Leave the household gear to me and Brenda," his princess-wife pretended to growl; "You go sharpen your brain or whatever it is you need to do!"

Tom nodded pleasantly and patted her on the royal backside. Then he went off to the Historian's Library at the windy top of Foretower. There *might* be information he could use in those thousands of musty old tomes and brittle hand-written parchments.

In Middletower Clem answered a knock on the door to their suite. Mistress Grumble, Murdan's Chatelaine, stood in the doorway, bearing a thick bundle of colorful fabrics.

"You all may need some needlework, Master Clematis," she said. "Cool cloth for the hot tropics, I should imagine."

"Of course!" called Mornie from the master bedroom. "We packed at home for winter at Overhall, not in Isthmusi. You guessed?"

"You must be very good at guessing, I guess," said Clem, "to be a castle-minder!"

"It doesn't hurt, you may believe me! Have you cool, loose dresses, Mistress? Have the boys brought swimming suits with them? No, Mistress Mornie, ma'am! No need to measure! Memorized *everybody's* sizes and shapes, waists, hips, heads and biceps, long since."

Furbetrance shook the last of the storm's crusted snow from his back and blew a blast of yellow fire over the top of the South Wall, melting the ice and evaporating it away entirely as a cloud of steam.

His brother joined him there.

"You'll have to find ol' Hoarling Frostbite in a mighty big snowfield. Sort of a needler in a haystack, isn't he?"

Retruance nodded. "I intend to ask around. Plenty of ptarmigans and fur seals and such up that way. I know a Beach Master among the walruses. He'll have some good ideas. A Dragon is hard to hide, especially in permafrosted places. Even if he is an Ice Dragon."

"I suppose. When will you leave, Brother?"

"Tom says he has some hours of research to do. And Manda is closeted with lots of heavy clothing, furs, leathers, thick threads and big needles. Even Manda can't whip together a half-dozen snow suits from scratch in a few minutes!"

"Are we—I mean—should you be in more of a hurry?"

"Murdan said it best. *Better prepared well than rush into battle half ready.*"

"I'll buy that." His brother laughed. "It's so much easier to be a Dragon! A bit of saltpeter and yellow sulfur between the cheek and the gum. Maybe some quarts of Tom's hot chili for the road!"

The Constable brothers lay on the top of the wall, simmering silently, watching the stars and the thin new moons. In the clear cold air and frozen landscape they picked out certain small snowbirds and tiny burrowing prairie dogs.

Small creatures often learn of danger long before Fairies, Elves, Witches or Wizards, Farmers or Soldiers—and even before Dragons. Good idea to stop and ask, now and again.

CHAPTER FOUR

Blackly Barguest

Sergeant Grey Grahamsson mustered the midnight watch between twelve-foot piles of dirty snow in Lower Bailey.

The storm clouds had cleared, leaving the sky ablaze with stars and two crescent moons. The air was bone-chilling cold, but very still.

The mid-watch of eight men huddled together, puffing clouds of vapor and shivering despite their heavy coats. Their stylish Overhall Guard uniforms were hidden under these rag-tag cold-weather vests and breaches.

These guys look just terrible! Grey thought to himself. *Dad would hand out demerits by the double handful!*

He shook his head sorrowfully but said nothing, just: "Hear me! Attention to orders!"

They were to patrol the tops of the outer walls in pairs, as always, keeping a sharp watch for night intruders or lost friends outside. Challenge anyone or anything approaching Overhall. Report same *at once* to the Officer of the Watch—himself—in a loud, clear hail.

"Attention! Fall out! Relieve the Watch!"

He hated his voice for cracking and squeaking in the cold air. *When will I develop a nice, loud, fearsome bellow like Dad's?*

Grey hitched up his broadsword and led the watch detail up the wall stairs at a trot, puffing. Once at the top, the Guardsmen split right and left, taking their positions and sending the grateful off-duty watch down to warm promises of hot tea, and bed.

Little was said. It was just too damn cold.

Shortly after midnight, a Guardsman named Willson hailed his officer.

"Something at the main gate, Corporal, sir!"

"*What* something, Willson?" Grey barked back.

"A big black dog, sir!"

"*Huh!* A black dog?"

"He wants in, sir! Looks pretty near froze!"

"O' course he's froze," Grey clucked sourly. "So aren't we all?"

The Main Gate, a thick, heavy, oak-and-iron-strap construction ten feet tall and twenty feet wide, was again heavily barred. To one side was a narrow door set into the same wall. To this Grey went, opened it, and followed a crooked passage to another heavy door in the outer wall.

"Well, come on in, whoever you be," he said pleasantly to the beast shivering without. "Shake off that snow as much as you can here! Stuff freezes to ice at a touch, you see, and clogs up the door hinges in a trice."

The big black dog did as asked and then trotted stiffly into the passageway between the doors.

"M-m-m-much b-b-better!" he panted.

He sat on his haunches and extended his right forepaw to the young officer. "Name's Blackly Barquest of Ramhold Station. Out on the Great Plains, you know?"

"Heard on it, o' course," the Corporal admitted. "Never been there, myself. Pretty long way away, I hears."

"You can say *that* again—and c-c-c-cold!"

"Come along, then! We'll get you warm and fed, old boy."

The big dog followed him across Lower Bailey to the stables, coops, byre, and kennels opposite the Guard quarters. The dog moved awkwardly on the freezing cobbles, limping painfully.

"Hurt, are you?"

"No, no! Just ice between me toes, y'see. Once I can dig it out I'll walk comfortable. Can a guy get a late bite, Colonel? Meals were few and far between in this weather."

He dug painful ice pellets from between his toes, groaning in relief all the while. Then he wolfed a huge portion of warmed-over roast goose from the castle kitchen, with day-old cornbread and cold suet pudding.

"A change from good old cold mutton, to be sure," he admitted. "Now, Commander, I'll get some rest. Do you think I'll be able to talk to the Lord Historian in the morning? Messages from Factor Talbert of Ramhold Late morning be soon enough, I judge."

"Sleep well, Blackly Barguest! I'll send word of you to Lord Historian and take you to him after breakfasting. It may be late, however, lots of departures early tomorrow morning."

"Well enough for ol' Blackly, General! Call me when Murdan pleases!"

He was asleep on a clean blanket not far from the sea coal fire before the young Guardsman had closed the door.

A diamond-clear, still morning dawned as Murdan, Tom Librarian, Woodsman Clem and their wives and children finished the early fast-breaking. The traveling parties prepared to depart by Dragon Flights on their fact-finding missions, north and south and east.

"Observe and report, for now," Murdan said for the fifth or sixth time.

"Never look for trouble if you can avoid it," laughed Tom. "If trouble is near, it'll come looking for you!"

"Do just as Daddy and Mama say," the Historian said gravely to the children.

"I am a *Princess!*" said Gay firmly. "I can take care of myself!"

"Keep an eye!" Murdan warned the parents with a twinkle in *his* eyes. "Remember that Hot Spell Arcolas taught you, Tom, my boy! A frozen Librarian won't be much use to his Princesses!"

He kissed the ladies, waved to the children and Brenda, shook hands once more with the boys, and waved them into the cleared area in Fore Bailey where their Dragons waited.

After attending to a dozen matters, most of them having to do with storm damage, Murdan stopped at the Foretower door and nodded to a Guardsman who waited to bespeak him.

"Lord Historian, a dog came in late last night—early this morning, really, sir. News from Factor Talbert at Ramhold. All is well there, he says."

"Send him up after lunch. I'm too old an Elf to stand around in these cold draughts!"

He patted the Guardsman on the shoulder and climbed the stairs to his suite—and blazing fire.

Some time later there was a knock, and the Guard brought in the large back dog, warmed, rested, and freshly brushed until his thick coat gleamed.

"Name's Blackly, m'lord Historian. Family of sheep dog called Barguest."

"You're from Ramhold, they tell me. How is Talbert doing in this weather? Everybody safe to home?"

"Yessir. Ramhold has some pretty fierce weather, winters *and* summers, as you probably know."

"And Talbert sent you. Pigeons not getting through the storm and the cold, of course."

"Lost *five* of 'em, brave little heroes. Frozen solid! Master Talbert thought I might have a better chance. Almost didn't make it. I close to froze meself, when I reached Overhall and scratched to get in."

"All thawed out now, however?"

"Fine as frog hair, Sir Historian! My report...?"

"Come sit with me by the fire, Blackly Barguest. You've had lunch?"

"A goodly start, at best," the dog admitted, plumping down as near to the roaring fire as he could safely get. "Sea coal? I could learn to love it, believe me."

"I'll send Ramhold a few hundredweight, soon as the roads are clear," Murdan promised. "You've earned it for yourself and your mates!"

"*Now!* What does Talbert have to say? Lost some lambs? Rams? Ewes? No Ramhold folk lost, please assure me."

"No, none of any, Historian! Talbert and his people—and a few of us faithful, fearless sheep dogs—managed to keep the flocks safe and warm, despite twenty feet of new snow over a foot of hard-packed ice we already had..."

"Twenty feet! We nearly died with twelve feet in twelve hours, here at home!"

"Master Talbert—we calls him 'Boss' but not to his face—says this blizzard was totally unexpected. Weather predicting on the Prairie is usually easy. You can usually see a storm a-coming for days before it hits."

"Interesting! Not quite as easy here, but—here it was quite unexpected, also."

"Master says, further: Moving colored lights in the northwest sky two nights before the storm. Aurora—not often seen in our latitudes, he says, but not entirely unknown."

"*Hmmm!* I see. We didn't notice 'em four or five nights ago, here."

"They're seen most often in the far sky, maybe a bit west of north. I saw them, myself. *Spooky!* Began at full dark and lasted until just before dawn, several nights in a row."

Murdan leaned back in his chair, lost in thought.

Blackly closed his eyes and laid his muzzle on his forepaws and waited.

Murdan arose and consulted a huge, leather-bound tome alone on a shelf above the fireplace.

"Northern Lights?"

"So some call 'em."

"They're seen not every year or every decade. Once or twice a century, it says here in *Starlight Revealed For What It Is.*"

He tapped the yellowed page, then closed the heavy binding and returned it to the shelf.

"Anything else, my friend?"

"Oh, the usual courteous greetings and business forecasts and such. He gave 'em in writing, which is very useful except I seem to have eaten a few of them when I got really hungry. I here have the rest, safe and sound."

"*If* I have any free time, now, for a long time. I must go speak to the King. What shall I do with you, Blackly?"

"You have something in mind, Historian, sir?" asked the dog without opening his eyes.

"*Um*, well—well, yes—I do. How do you feel about Dragons?"

"Never met one I didn't like. On the other hand, I've never met one, at all."

"You will! I'll send you home…"

"I was just getting to like it here," the sheepdog protested, half joking.

"…and maybe further than that. It depends. But first let me get a-hold of a certain lazy, ancient, duty-shirking, slow-moving fireplug…"

"A horse?"

"*No! My* Dragon."

"*Uh!*—We dogs prefer to walk, you know."

"No time!"

He muttered a string of words Blackly didn't quite catch. As the dog watched, trying hard not to look surprised nor overly impressed, the Historian listened and said, quite clearly, "Good, then! Hurry!"

He rose from his chair and began pulling shirts and under-drawers from highboys and stuffing a large leather saddlebag he'd yanked from under his bed.

"I've called Arbitrance—*my* Dragon. He's visiting his daughter-in-law over on the west coast. They can be here by noon tomorrow."

"That's fast flying, I guess. And we are going to fly somewhere? Somewhere *beyond* Ramhold?"

"No, no! *I'm* going to Lexor by Arbitrance. *You'll* be flown to Ramhold by Hetabelle, Furbetrance's wife. You don't know Furbie, of course, but don't worry! Hetabelle is a great gal in every way."

Blackly sat watching Murdan, skillfully assisted by a company of maids and manservants, hunting and fetching, pressing and mending and arguing about this coat or that cummerbund or those boots.

The Historian was, after all, going to Court.

"I've asked my Arbitrance to talk to his son Furbetrance, *en route*. Dragons can do that, you know. Tom and Manda and Retruance are to wait for you at Ramhold. To hear my news and my opinions and, I hope, to accompany them further westward. Dragons are great but you dogs are special in your own way in snow. Better get some sleep. The hearth here is best, I think. Be around for breakfast and our departures."

He patted the big black dog on the head and scratched behind his ears, then went off to try to sleep a while, himself.

Blackly heard him say fondly: "Nice dog! Good puppy!"

Tom, Manda, Gay, and a wildly excited Brenda, aboard Retruance Constable that night landed at Ramhold, met with joy and celebration.

Clem, Mornie and their half-grown lads on Furbetrance spent the night at the isolated Waterfield's farm of Martin and Phoebe and their daughter Katy in a somewhat warmer but wetter climate.

CHAPTER FIVE
Exeunt

An early riser, the big black dog let himself out of the Historian's suite and trotted down the wide stair to explore a bit before breakfast.

Castle youngsters, also early risers despite the intense cold, dashed up to get acquainted with this stranger in their midst.

"Are you a kind of *Dragon?*" one little girl asked. "Or some sort of raving monster like that? How horrible you must be!"

"No, I'm just a simple shepherd dog from Ramhold Station. Do you pups know about Ramhold?"

"I know! *I know!*" cried a tousle-headed lad. "Me Pa tells tales of Ramhold! "Way out in the desert, he says."

"Desert? Well, I guess your Pa might think so. What does he do, tell me?"

"He's the best dairyman in all Overhall. Tends the Lord's milk herd, and makes cream for his oatmeal, you know, and butter for Baker Cleland's best biscuits! And there's smelly cheeses, too!"

"He's much too big-mouthed 'bout his Pa's work," a little girl said with a sniff. "*I* can brag, too! *My* father's Chief of Hatcheries, Runs and Roosts."

"Fancy that!" laughed the dog. "Chickens is among my favorites! Hello! What's the bell? Breakfast call?"

"Breakfast!" the children shouted. "Let's eat!"

"Go on ahead," Blackly told them. "I'm to break fast with Lord Murdan. So he told me last night."

Before he could add anything further, the children disappeared in the direction of the Dining Hall beneath Foretower.

"I *thought* I heard your bark," came a new voice. "Lord Historian is up and dressed and about to break his fast."

"*Ah!* You're the young soldier who let me in from the cold this morning. I forgot to get your name. Or give you thanks for saving me from freezing solid!"

"I be Greysolon, Corporal of Overhall Guards. Always helpful to friends," his savior winked, "as well as beat the tar out of enemies. Come along, Blackly Barquest. Murdan awaits!"

"Everybody's off, already, except you and me, Blackly," Murdan told the dog while dishing out a generous serving of bacon and scrambled eggs. "You've luggage?"

"Not me! I travels light."

"Then I'll order that sea coal I promised you. Mistress Hetabelle won't mind the extra cargo. We're about ready to leave. Corporal?"

"Aye, Historian?"

"Prepare to load Dragons. We'll leave at once. The sooner..."

"...the best, m'lord!" the Guardsman finished, saluting.

"Fifteen minutes, give-or-take a minute, Corporal. Take a plate of eggs for yourself. Man works better with a full cargo."

Blackly mumbled around a large gulp of hot, salted, peppered and crisply fried potatoes. "Good as at home."

"Ready?" Murdan called, when he and Blackly stepped out into Foretower Bailey.

"Yessir, Historian!" rumbled the vast grey and black Dragon named Arbitrance Constable.

"Good lizard! *Now!* Meet Madame Hetabelle, Blackly. She's the wife of Arbitrance. All set, then? Keep under the furs, young pup. The faster a Dragon flies, the colder you'll feel."

The day was clear and sharp and the furs draped between Hetabelle's rear ears were very welcome. The lady Dragon said little until she had climbed a thousand feet above Overhall Ridge and turned west.

"Now, then!" she at last said, glancing back at her passenger. "Blackly, is it? From Ramhold? We Dragons tend to avoid places like Ramhold.

Frighten the poor little lambs, we do so easily!"

"N-n-not surprising. Most sheep never see anything bigger'n a pied pony, all lifetime," the dog agreed a bit shakily. "You must forgive me if I'm scared almost out of me wits! Never flew anywhere or anybody, before."

"I understood and forgive," the Dragon-mother chuckled kindly.

Blackly decided she was quite nice, despite her fearsome display of white teeth, black wings, sharp green claws and shocking pink scales. He wagged his tail in thanks—deep under the furs.

"You kits!" shouted the lady with a spout of purplish smoke that smelled of sulfur and geraniums. "Keep up, now. We're going to fly *really* fast to not keep Uncle Retruance waiting overlong."

Blackly turned about to see four much smaller Dragonfolk following Hetabelle and he grunted—barked, actually—in surprise.

"Sorry! I should have introduced my children before we took off."

The four Dragonettes grinned at him broadly and dipped a wing each when their mother named them.

"In mint green is my eldest. Her name is Bravura…"

"We calls her Brass Nose," said the second of the kits.

"Only as long as she permits it," Hetabelle growled good-naturedly. "Tell the nice doggy what she calls *you*, Gonerell."

"Oh, she calls me Gorgonzola, most times."

"And your little sisters?"

"This is Chartreuse. Say '*Pleased to meet you!*' Charlie, dear!"

"Pleased!" said the next smallest maiden Dragonette, blushing even pinker than her mother.

The fourth and smallest daughter swept forward to greet the dog. "I calls meself Blue. Everybody else calls me Little Blue. I can bark like a dog, too! It comes out as sort of a greenish-yellow smoke!"

"Good girl, Miss Blue!" Blackly laughed aloud. "I understand to call your sister Charlie, with her permission, I'm very pleased to meet you all."

"There's another," insisted Brass Nose. "There's Brazier. He's my twin brother. He went to find Princess Amanda and Princess Gay and Sir Thomas!"

"So he did," Hetabelle said proudly. "Social amenities taken care of, it's time to fly fast as we can. Stay real close up. Don't wander off *any*, Little Blue!"

She lifted her powerful black pinions and snapped them down so they cracked like giant whips. Her children shot after her, trailing pale streaks of colored smoke.

Blackly settled deep in his furs on Hetabelle's broad head. He found it quite safe and comfortable and perhaps even a little *too* warm. He watched the snow-covered plain shoot beneath and fell asleep.

Fifty miles east and a third of the way to Lexor, the Historian was giving vent to his uncertainty and apprehension.

Arbitrance—good, old, patient Constable that he usually was—listened with his after-left ear. He'd carried and helped and advised and listened to Murdan for more than a century, and knew his moods and salty language quite well.

"Are you *listening?*" Murdan demanded.

"Most carefully, my dear Companion. Quite closely! Have you reached a full stop? Pray tell me where we're going, more specifically. Lexor is rather a big place!"

Murdan's fuming died away at the Dragon's calming words—and the need to catch his breath.

"I apologize, Arbitrance! Arcolas says 'tis healthier to get the cursing and screaming out of the way so one can think."

"Where?" his mount repeated patiently.

"Ah, well—I expect the King is at Sweetwater Tower for the holidays. We perhaps should stop by Amanda Alone Palace first to make sure. Ask somebody. Fastest that way."

"You realize we'll reach the city before dawn?"

"That'd put us at Sweetwater before breakfast. Give my half-brother Eduard time to wake himself."

The Dragon resisted a strong urge to shrug, which could have been dangerous for the Royal Historian on his head, and increased his air speed, instead.

"I still wonder where that blasted Arcolas has gone," muttered Murdan.

"They may know at Sweetwater. Arcolas has many friends around the capital," his Dragon suggested.

It had been part of his job for many years to calm a fiery Historian.

Tom didn't mind a delay at Ramhold when he received the message carried by the young Brazier.

Murdan's thriving wool-gathering business, run by Factor Talbert and a dozen shepherds and shepherdesses plus a few specialists—veterinarians, wranglers and a cooking staff—made them most welcome. New faces and new voices, new songs and stories, were as important to people living in the middle of vast grasslands as food and drink.

Brenda at first held back, shy of these rough, tough and boisterous plainspeople, but in a few hours she was mingling, talking, singing, eating and dancing with them like an old friend.

Gay, who knew them all by name, ancestry, children, parents, dogs, and even their stocky ponies, felt right at home.

"If Hetabelle moves as fast as I know she can, she should be here before suppertime," Tom said to the Factor. "Tell us all you can about this early blizzard. Murdan seems to feel it wasn't a *natural* storm."

"I thought as much when we saw the Sky Lights."

"Well, you know as much as we do." Tom reached for a second cup of rich shepherd's coffee. "Possibly Murdan has sent further information with Hetabelle. He thought seriously enough of Clem's news to go to Lexor to tell Eduard."

"All respect to the Woodsman." Talbert nodded. "He's nobody's fool."

Like most inland dwellers, Talbert thought seamen and traders who plied the open seas were either twisted in mind or crooked in heart. Or both.

"Clem says his friend is credible," Manda pointed out.

"*Creditable,* rather—but yes," her husband agreed.

"What will you do, then, Librarian? Stay here as long as you need or want, of course."

"Thank you, Factor! We'll see what Dame Hetabelle has to add. I think we must go to Wall, though. What's beyond Wall is still a mystery to us all. Rumors on speculations; no more. We don't even know who the enemy might be..."

"Terrible high snowfall? Deep cold and wind? Someone worse than the old Rellings, I fear."

"...*if* an enemy, at all. Well, we'll take a look and see if we can find out what it's all about."

"Expect the worst, says I. Take some of us with you for safety, Tom. Things will be quiet here until spring thaw."

Tom considered this offer but said, "No, Talbert. With great thanks, but Carolna needs solid information, not a show of force. Besides, there's not Dragon-headroom enough."

❧❧

Blackly studied the smooth white landscape below as Hetabelle and her children skimmed the prairie.

"Not much in the way of landmarks," he muttered aloud. "This fast and this high? I can't get much from the scents from here."

"I fly by the stars and they're very clear, as sun goes down. I'll teach you celestial navigation, if we have time."

"Steer by moons and stars? Make me a better dog than most of us sheep herders."

"Mama," came a call from behind. "Mama! The little ones are tiring, I fear. Not me! I can go a long ways yet."

"Bravura, my dear, I understand. We're almost there and soon will set down at Ramhold. Please keep up and inward!"

"Yes, Mama," came four answers.

"Good girls! Maybe fifteen more minutes!"

As the sun disappeared below the western horizon, the shepherds of Ramhold lit three great bon fires, showing where the ranch complex lay hidden beneath the snow cover.

"Stay close. Land softly! You might crack a toe on a roof below, otherwise!" Hetabelle warned.

And they dropped from the dark sky into the unbroken whiteness.

"Welcome to Ramhold!" came Tom's voice from a swirl of loose snow and sharp bits of ice. "Hit it just right!"

"My job is hitting things just right, Librarian! Here's everybody, including a nice sheep dog who lives here. Children? Say polite "hello" to the good knight! Master Blackly? Meet Sir Thomas, Librarian of Overhall...?"

"Call me Tom! Ramhold is no place for honorary titles."

"As feel we all of Ramhold, Tom," said Blackly. "I've flown home to help you go north. Can we go down inside, now? I swear, it must be well below zero, right here on the bunkhouse roof!"

CHAPTER SIX
The Beast in the Lake

Clem folded his heavy bearskin coat, much too warm since early that morning, and wedged it into a saddlebag behind Furbetrance's after-left rear ear.

"Getting mighty warm," he said to Mornie. "If you want to change for cooler, we can land."

"No, I've been over these wetlands before and I dressed by layers for their weather this morning. And the boys, too."

"Well and good, woman! But it will turn dark in less than an hour. Pick us a dry spot, if you can find one."

The Woodsman and his wife, their two young sons and Furbie, searched the seemingly endless wetlands.

"*Lake!* Lake *there!* Big island, too!" shouted both Gregor and Thomas at the same time—loudly enough to startle Furbetrance,

"*Ah!* It's where Father Arbitrance hid himself a while. Above flood levels, as I recall."

"A garden in a wasteland!" Mornie cried. "I see roses, and—*yes!*—looks like oranges and lemons! We could spend the night here safely, I think."

"We will—although the story of Arbitrance's sojourn—is that the right word, Mornie? Sojourn?—was real sad, actually."

"We can land dry, build a nice fire and you can tell us campfire stories afterwards," young Thomas suggested.

Furbetrance tilted steeply down to the unruffled turquoise lake and the lush green island where his father, enchanted at the time, had held a

Prince Royal as his captive.

"Plenty wood to burn," Tommy said. "And the shelter still has a roof!"

"Maybe few things needing doing," his father agreed as he swung his boys down from the Dragon's off knee. "We'll do it! I'll start a fire and supper. Mother, sort out the bedding, please. You young woodpeckers take a look around with Furbetrance, but don't get further than a whistle. There be dangerous critters in these waters at times."

The boys, followed more slowly by the Dragon, dashed excitedly off to the lakeshore and the still lagoon.

"Let's swim!" Tommy shouted. "Last one in's a dumb brother!"

He hardly paused to shed his jeans and shirt, but it gave the Dragon time to catch up with them.

"Half a moment, youngsters! Let me check before you dive in."

"Oh, don't be a piffle, Furbie! It's warm enough. C'mon, big brother!"

"I says 'wait!' and I means 'stop all engines,' " Arbitrance snorted. "I like a cool dip as much as anybody, but …"

He shot his head forward past the boys at the water's edge.

There came a terrific crash, a series of loud, wet splashes, and a two-toned bellow shook the palmettos at the top of the beach.

Clem came dashing through the orchard, waving a large soup ladle over his head.

"Wha' huh! Here a Woodma, righ' on cue," Furbie mumbled, his mouth being full. *"Can y' tell us wha' we've caugh'?"*

Clem slid to a halt in shallow water and leaned far over to examine the Dragon's captive.

"Well, they don't run much in my North Woods," he decided, "but I guess maybe a crocodile? Or is he an alligator? About ten feet long at that! Speak for yourself, beastie!

"Not a cayman, are ye? I hear them cayman are *really* hardest to catch. I'll just keep a claw on your neck…to support you, sort of, *eh?*"

"He came sneaking up on us *under water!*" Gregor cried.

"Nay! Just watching. Out of curiosity, only."

"He's got a point there," puffed Clem, sticking the long spoon in his belt. "What were his intentions? You did perfectly a-right, Furbetrance

Constable."

"One of those—*ah!*—fearsome Constable Dragon, are ye? Welcome to Dragon's Hummock, then, good sir."

"You knew my dear father, then?"

"Not too well, sir. We 'gators tended to stay clear of him."

The party moved across the beach and walked to the shelter, a hundred paces inland.

"A *crocodile!*" squeaked Mornie, dropping a bolt of mosquito netting. "Oh, dear!"

"No, Mama. This is an *alligator*. He hasn't yet told us his name, yet," Gregor said.

"My humble apologies, ma'am! I am called DuWitt. I'm native of these waters. I'm sorry I gave your menfolk that bad start."

"Are you hungry, DuWitt?" the practical Mornie asked. "I mean, we haven't a great deal to share. We're merely spending a night."

"Never mind, dear lady. I ate well and full not four days back. A taste here. A nibble there? I'll be a good guest at your campfire, I promise."

Despite the threatening beginning, supper proceeded in as friendly a manner as could be expected. Furbetrance lay close beside the alligator, keeping eyes skinned for any false moves.

DuWitt lay very still except to snap up odd bits and slices of the meat course the boys offered out of curiosity as well as their natural friendliness.

"It'll get cold, here, shortly—even beside this nice fire," the alligator said at last. "I should return to the water soon. Us 'gators tend to go rather torpid when the sun goes down."

"I'll walk you back to your mudbank, then," Furbetrance offered. "Whenever you're ready."

"Well, ready am I, I guess. You're very kind, Noble Dragon!"

The 'gator yawning mightily—and toothily—crawled beside the Dragon in the direction of the beach.

"Nice bunch, these Herronssons. Good commons, even for a great Dragon such as you."

"Or an Alligator—like *you*. Continue to behave yourself, DuWitt, m'boy. Here's your bed. We'll be gone in the morning."

"Oh—well! So be it. One last thing, Dragon. Please tell Master Clem this warm weather will continue for several days…"

"Will it? We had twelve feet of snow, up at Overhall three days back!"

"Not here," the 'gator insisted after another vast yawn. "G'night! Good journey, Dragon."

He slipped into the sticks, leaves, palm fronds and warm wet mud of his shelter.

Chapter Seven
Snowbound Canyon

"As far as can be told from here," said the Ramhold Factor, shedding his heavy wool jacket, "the snow is deep and the air is colder than ever, here and all around."

"How far did *you* scout?" Tom asked Retruance, who had his head just inside the double door of the Hall.

"Same story for two hundred miles—and ever colder as you go north and west, Companion."

"Perhaps better if Retruance and I go on alone," Tom said to Manda.

"I disagree! We'll be far better off with you, husband, and two—no, six—fiery Dragons, as cold as it might get!"

"But our daughter? Not to mention Brenda?"

"We'd have to either leave them here—or send them back to Overhall. Which would mean sending Hetabelle and her kits, too."

The discussion—argument—went on into the cold, clear night.

"My Ramhold Station is probably as safe as anywhere," Talbert insisted. "We're prepared for a lot more winter weather, here."

"But can you—er?—evacuate? If a flying or sliding enemy came?"

"Well..." was all the Factor could say. "I just don't know, Lady Manda. Just don't know."

Near midnight, Manda stood and said, firmly, "My child is better off with her father and with me! She *will* go with us.

Tom gestured to his Dragon, who had remained silent during the long discussion.

Retruance slowly nodded his great, green head.

"I have to agree with Manda, in the end."

Tom shrugged and nodded to his wife.

"Right! We'll leave for Hidden Lake after breakfast, then. Go on to Wall the next day, if everything is right at our Achievement."

Soft snow evenly blanketed the bottom of the steep-sided canyon, hiding everything normally as landmarks. Yet, a thin line of blue-grey smoke rose from a tall snowbank at the head of the frozen lake.

"*Someone* is alive," Tom called to Manda. "They haven't started to dig out yet, I guess."

"Why should they? Everything they might need for a week or two or more is in the house."

"Retruance? Make a noise to warn them of our coming."

The Dragon snorted pinkish smoke and opened his mouth to emit a dragon-roar that echoed and re-echoed from the walls of the canyon.

"Someone—coming from the second storey windows. Looks like Julia!" he said.

From Canyon House came the high, snarling, shrill sound of a jaguar's cry. Several elfin figures came tumbling after her from the window of the Dining Hall, sliding gleefully down a pile of snow and calling out in relief and in greeting.

"Looks like you survived all this, I'd say," Manda called as Retruance lowered his head to greet the house staff and Julia.

"No problem," the big cat purred. "We're used to bad weather, out here. Not usually quite so cold. I came inside to keep the little folks company, you see. Besides, most game is hiding deep under the drifts. And the water has frozen hard and deep on lake and stream."

"Froze all the water?" Tom asked.

"The pipes we set deep enough to keep from freezing, as you planned, sir," reported Friddle, their *Major Domo*. "Our only worry was what was happening elsewhere. It obviously was a terribly widespread storm. A real blizzard!"

"It certainly was that. We heard it laid down many feet of drifts from here all the way to Lexor," Tom told the servants. "Not all reports were in yet when we started westward. Anything else to report?"

"No," said Julia, leading the crowd back inside the Dining Hall window.

"Animals were gathered to folds and barns and stables in time, fortunately."

"Miss Julia felt the blizzard coming in her bones," one of the house-maids said in an awed tone. "We owe her a whole lot!"

"Of course, you do, my dear," the Jaguar laughed. "What do you all say to some early dinner, Princess Manda?"

"Come along, girls. We'll supervise. Bison steaks, I suggest. Give Julia time to tell Daddy all about our deep freeze."

"Yes, Mama," said the little Princess, pausing only to stroke the Jaguar's thick, soft fur.

Julia had always been a great favorite with her.

"The livestock, bless 'em, may not be very smart but smart enough to come in out of a storm," Friddle was saying. "Not true of chickens, how-ever. Load of the hens froze on their nests. We'll have fried and broiled and baked and stewed hen for the rest of the winter, I suspect. And a shortage of eggs for a few weeks."

"Still, I'm relieved. As isolated as we are here!"

Manda perched on a three-legged stool beside the vast kitchen work-table, making lists of things in short supply and things needing to be done.

"Eggs we can do without until the pullets start laying in the springtime," she told Hilda, her Chief Cook. "Plenty of flour, you tell me. Bread and pancakes and muffins to keep you all from starving. How about butter, I wonder?"

"As long as our cows are contented, they'll give us milk and butter and cheese," Hilda said. "Good old bossies! Dependable is the word for them, all."

"Let me see, then. Coffee? Tea? Cocoa? Wine and ale in plenty, I suppose?"

"Plenty of them all, Princess. A few luxuries we lack and will until the supply barges can get down the river and the oxen trains up from Whitehead Landing. Might be months!"

"I don't need to tell you to keep close tabs on stores, Cookie. Tom and I and Retruance will be going on to Wall shortly. You'll be on your own for a long while."

"If I could ask a small favor, Princess? The fore and after courtyards are under twelve feet of ice and snow. It'll take all the men and some of us ladies, too, a week to shovel and chip it up...?"

"Talk to Retruance. He and his nephew can melt everything away and dry the melt-water, too, in a couple of hours, I should think."

"*We'll* go ask him," piped Gay, jumping down from her stool. "C'mon

Brenda! It'll be great fun to *shoose* the snow."

Shoosing the courtyards, sidewalks, terraces, roofs, roadways and paths, not to mention horse paddocks and cattle feeding yards, plus all the related chores that had to be done to make Hidden Canyon House safe, dry, and comfortable once more, took them five full days.

In the meantime, the cold continued, although no more snow fell.

"I fear a sudden melt," Tom said to his wife. "Think of the flooding!"

"As a farmer's boy you should know that farms are designed to take care of themselves in spring floods and summer storms. Don't worry."

"What worries me is this cold. It hasn't climbed above minus ten degrees all week! At this rate it may take all summer to melt all the snow and ice away, once it does warm up!"

Manda came over and sat on his lap to hug him fiercely.

"You fear all this is unnatural? Is magically created?"

"I don't know."

"A lot of people everywhere, I suspect, are worried about it. Is Carolna under attack, already, without realizing it? And by whom? Or what?

"We'll be closer to *whatever* it is when we get to Wall," her husband sighed. "We leave Thursday morning, beautiful Princess. Unless you've changed your mind about going further?"

"No, as wife, mother and Princess, I must go along."

"And Gay? She'd be quite safe and happy here."

Manda was silent for a long minute, but then shook her head.

"No. If there's danger to one of us, there's danger to *all* of us, no matter where we hide away. Gay will be safer with us."

Tom nodded reluctantly but gave her a kiss.

CHAPTER EIGHT
Two if by Sea

"It would be better, I think," Retruance said, "if we would fly by night. With bright sunlight and full snow coverage below, even Dragons will have trouble seeing landmarks clearly."

"We'd not see much, day *or* night, as long as the snow covers everything," Tom considered. "We want speed to Wall. We'll continue in daylight, I say."

"You're the thinker of the party, Companion," the great beast agreed.

He spread the Dragon Flight out in a long right-to-left line. He held the middle while Hetabelle flew fifty wing-lengths to his right and young Brazier flew as far to the left.

Two Dragonettes flew just within sight beyond their mother and a third beyond her brother. Baby Blue stayed, on strict orders from Mama Hetabelle, a few yards directly behind her mother.

"Eyes open and sharp!" Hetabelle instructed her kits. "Never out of sight, but far out as you can get. Make a red smoke puff and a loud yell if you see something. Understand?"

"Yes, Mama!" the Dragonettes chorused.

"This way we'll cover a hundred-mile swath, you see," Retruance explained to Manda. "Let's get aloft, Constables!"

They flew a compass course due northwest at two thousand feet, swiftly—Tom figured their air speed was in the neighborhood of a hundred miles an hour—each element falling slightly behind and a little below Retruance, who bore Manda, Tom, the little girls and Blackly.

"We'll make Wall before nightfall." Tom was sure.

"If we can *find* Wall—or even see the sea when we get to it," Manda growled back. She, Gay and Brenda sat with their backs to the westering sun and the wind, looking behind and below the Dragon Flight.

"Don't get discouraged, now, Princess, "Hetabelle called. "I see there're some dark clouds low on the western horizon. They should give us some relief if we have to search for Wall."

Manda nodded sleepily and tucked thick furs around her shoulders and over the girls, who were actually asleep close beside her. Despite the frigid airs blustering about them, the Dragon's inner heat kept them quite comfortable.

Tom sneezed loudly and accepted a flask of steaming coffee the Dragon handed up to him from some hidden hot pocket. Tom filled his cup, gulped the contents eagerly, then turned to hand the flask to Manda, only to find she, too, had fallen asleep.

"Well, she must be fairly comfortable if she can nap."

And he and his Companion drank the rest of the coffee.

The last half-cup had already turned cold.

Five days earlier, Murdan had handed a cup of tea to his half-brother, the King of Carolna, as he sat up in the royal bed.

Eduard sipped cautiously and then said, "Go ahead!"

"Not much information beyond that, I'm afraid. We'll hear from Tom and Clem, soon. Perhaps. What can *we* do, now?"

Eduard considered a long moment.

"Alert the army, right off. Order Ffallmar to call up the Achievement Reserves—somewhere! In Lexor, I should imagine. Has it stopped snowing?"

"Since midnight—but it's *awfully* cold, now. Troops will have trouble moving anywhere until they clear some roads."

"The navy, bless 'em, is frozen solid at anchor, I understand, except for a few ships laying-to in open Brantwater. Goodness knows what's happened to my ships at sea!"

Eduard slid himself out of bed and called for his valet to bring small clothes, trousers and a shirt.

"We'll break our fast, first, Historian Then do what we can think of to prepare for—whatever will come. Tell Walden to bring my Wizard

Council—the ones here at Lexor—to a meeting at noon. Some of them may have ideas who's causing this foul weather."

"I wish I knew where Arcolas is," Murdan muttered. "Have Walden ask around for him, will you? Some of the wizardly crew you keep here may know."

"At once. Pass the cream! If nothing else we can help the storm-bound and hungry. Come in, my dear! Have a bite with us and help plan for this emergency!"

This was a greeting to Queen Beatrix who entered, looking both beautiful and anxious. Word of the great blizzard was spreading quickly

"Good morning, my dear!" Murdan said, helping her to a seat. "We seem to be facing some emergency, here. And we can't even tell, yet, what it is!"

"To me that sounds like the ordinary daily life for our King," the Queen laughed. "I just looked out at my garden and it's deep under his snow! It never snows like this down at Knollwater. Very beautiful! But also very cold!"

General Woodruffle of the Carolna Army ordered his five hundred soldiers, armed with shovels and brooms and such weather tools, out into the snow and ice that smothered The Point.

"We are under the King's order to muster all troops," he explained to his sleepy subordinates. "And we can't do *that* until we get rid of this damned snow here. Get 'em going! I want Parade clear and dry by noon! Go! *Go!*"

At anchor in Brant Bay, frozen solid in ice four feet thick, its rigging thrumming uneasily in the light breeze, lay HMS *Muriel*. Her doughty commanding officer, a bluff, hearty Captain Witherspoon, climbed down a rope ladder from her port taffrail, almost fell on his backside when he slipped on the ice and, followed by half-dozen officers, managed to skate away from *Muriel's* side twenty yards or so before he jiggled, juggled and finally halted, causing a ragged crunch of his senior men grasping each other to keep erect.

"This ice runs a fathom thick!" someone cried, rather in awe than fear. "Take a week of warm winds to work 'em free, Capt'n!"

"We should send the crews ashore, sir," another suggested. "If this ice gets to shifting about by stronger winds, it'll crush our hulls like eggshells!"

The Captain, an old sea hand, examined the scene, the trapped ships and the expanse of glare ice swept clear of loose snow here.

"*No!* We'll save 'em, Gods willing! Break out shovels, picks and plows; see if we have some plows below. I want a channel cleared out to that open middle area!"

He started back to the flagship, and the younger men followed, whispering to each other anxiously.

"You swabs look like a pack of penguins waddling about on this ice. Come on! At least we'll try!" their Captain snarled.

Arms waving, stamping bare feet on the hot sand and calling greetings to Clem and his family and to Furbetrance, the Parvaiti came running to meet them, lead by a wizened old man in a grass skirt and a frown of red ginger blossoms, freshly gathered.

"Hail, Woodsman! Greetings to you, Lady Mornie and stout Clemsson lads! Welcome to East Pelehoehoe, Furbetrance Constable!" the villagers sang.

"Greetings to you, friends! Hello, Tiki Byron!" the boys yelled back.

They were encircled by loving arms, kissed and hugged and patted and giggled over, as they dismounted.

"You are recovered from your sad mishap?" Byron asked Clem. "We heard about it days ago and have worried about it ever since."

"Recovered, now," Clem chuckled. "We come to your warm shore and jungle to complete my cure. Bad weather up North! Let me tell you…"

"Come up to Long House, first. Cool drinks and hot lunch, shortly. Go ahead and play with my young people, then, Clemssons. Plenty of lemon and lime and orange and pineapple juice to drink when you get hot and sandy!"

The Parvaiti were a happy and sometimes noisy tribe, which made them good company for visitors—except at a meal, where they devoted their time and attention to eating and enjoying.

Once the luncheon began things got much quieter and Clem spoke to the Tiki. Byron Boldface seldom these days wore the huge, hot, fierce teakwood mask that once gave him his surname.

"*Two* reasons for our coming, Tiki," Clem began. "I needed a bit of rest in warm weather. Dreadfully cold, up north. Snow—do you know what I mean by snow?"

"I have heard of it. Saw it once, when I was a sailor, myself, a century back."

"Grips the entire northland this wintertime! It almost killed me! But that's a story for long warm evenings here on your beach."

"We await it with great eagerness, Woodsman."

"I'm to ask your thinking about a possible enemy, perhaps, coming out of the far north of Hintoo, somewhere and somehow. We don't have a name for this enemy, yet, but wiser heads than mine fear the extreme cold and heavy snows that have closed our world tight arise from evil spells."

"Tell me from the beginning," said the old man, settling his hips more comfortably. "As far as I know, I'm the only person on this continent who's ever lived long and traveled much in Hintoo."

"There're only a few scattered Snowmen tribes up beyond the Hintoo frost line," Byron said after he'd heard the details of the possible invasion. "I don't think any of them have the power to control the weather, as you seem to suggest. If they did, I would think they would warm it up at home, rather than send it against others. It doesn't make sense to me, Clematis."

"Nor to me, but I was told to ask. You are, as you say, the only one who's wandered inland on the other side of the Peaceful. Sailors and traders only get to the seaports, usually."

"Making rain—let alone snow and freezing winds—takes a great deal of magical muscle," Byron added, shaking his head. "It has to be somebody else. Or perhaps the weather you have suffered is just natural phenomenon?"

"I've never seen a winter like this one, Tiki."

"My lad, I have lived—what?—four time longer than you. Five times? I've seen a lot more weather than most. More even than our honored Historian, my friend Murdan. "

Clem nodded slowly.

"I must get your thoughts to Murdan. But messenger pigeons can't fly into the cold and snow."

"There are beasts to call upon we can send anywhere, as long as it's reached by water. Unfrozen water, preferably. Sea turtles and porpoises… *but no!* There is Florenz Sea Dragon. He would know how to reach Lexor."

"Tom's in Wall by now. I don't know if that coast is open."

"We can only try. And maybe we get a message to our good friend

Florenz Stillacho McNess. You remember Flo?

"Very well!" Clem cried. "He helped us escape from your volcano when it blew up! Where is he?"

"Traveling. Studying ocean currents. He was kind enough to give us a way to call him, in case of need. I will do it at dawn tomorrow. And talk to some porpoises and turtles, too. Prepare messages about our talk, Woodsman. Two to Tom at Wall. Two for the King at Lexor. One for the Sea Dragon to carry. Copies for the porpoises and turtles."

"And then…we'll just have to sit in the warm sun and wait." Clem sighed.

CHAPTER NINE
One of Our Maidens is Missing!

"Where's Wall!" groaned Tom, shielding his eyes against the flaring sun, setting behind the dark horizon clouds. "Is this a snowfield?—or is it the open sea covered with ice?"

Retruance replied. "I think we're somewhere between Wall and Herron's Mill."

"It soon will be dark—and I imagine the young Dragonettes are getting tired," Manda said over her shoulder. "We should land, eat something, and hole up for the night."

Before either her husband or his Dragon could reply, there was a shrill whistle from Brass Nose at the far, northern end of the Line of Flight.

"*Smoke!* Somebody down there, Librarian!"

"Might be a fisherman's shore cottage—or it *might* be Herron's homestead—Clem's Papa's mill?"

Their Line of Flight swung gracefully down toward several regularly-shaped mounds of snow under a stand of snow-bowed pines.

"Herron's Mill, for sure," Retruance called. "See the water wheel!"

"And there's Herron and there's Clem's mother Lily!" Tom called back. "Hello the Mill! Permission to land!"

"Right ye are, Tom Librarian!" came Herron's deep voice through the still evening air. "Come on in! We have barn and stables warm for our creatures and there's still plenty of room for all you Constables!"

Woodsman-turned-miller Herron and his cheery, plumpish wife Lily kept most of their grown children close to home.

Daughters Rose and Azalea each had married and produced a dozen lively grandchildren between them. Their husbands had worked at the mill before they married—and remained in Herron's employ as captains of timber schooners.

Of their five sons, eldest Clematis (known as Clem) had gone into the deep northern forests to trap furs—until he met Tom and later married Mornie, Princess Manda's Maid of Honor.

Hibiscus (called Hi for short), Columbine (Col) and Portulaca (Port) brought their wives to live at their father's mill, but the youngest Herrons-son, Narcissus (Cus) had gone to sea years ago and was seldom heard from, except for gifts at the midwinter Holiday Season.

"The last came just a day or two before the early snow," Lily told Manda as they prepared supper. "A beautiful robe of silk for me! Too good for most mornings, but I wear it for Papa, now and again, when we're alone."

"Let me see it. Ah, it came from the Far West, I think. I saw jumpers just like this in pictures of Hintoo ladies. Exquisite women and dressed so luxuriously!"

"He must have bought this robe across the sea, somewhere, then." Lily sighed. "I would much rather have had himself."

"Of course! He'll appear on your doorstep one of these mornings, dear Lily. Shall I smash these potatoes?"

"Papa prefers them sliced and fried crisp in bacon fat, Princess. Do you mind?"

"I only mind you calling me 'Princess.' " Manda laughed. "I'm simply 'Manda,' the wife of Thomas the Overhall Librarian!"

"Call *me* whatever you like as long as it's to dinner!" Tom joked from across the huge family room.

"What should we feed these here Dragons?" Herron asked with a worried frown. "Seven of 'em! That big a critter must down a whole cargo of vittles every mealtime."

"Dragons eat far less than you'd think, actually." Tom reassured him. "They'll eat just about anything!"

"Even boys and girls?" Brenda asked Gay.

The girls were seated with Blackly (who was pretending to be asleep) on the wide hearth, soaking up welcome warmth and toasting marshmallows.

"Who can tell?" Gay teased. "Don't be 'fraid! The secret is to keep Dragons fed on what they *really* like."

"Which is...what?"

"Oh—pancakes with lots of butter and maple syrup and pork sausages, Mama says. And green olives stuffed with red pim—pim—red peppers."

"Yuck!" Brenda objected. *"Green* olives!"

The shepherd's dog listened to them, silently chuckling but not opening his eyes.

"Little girls!" he thought. "Alike everywhere. Love 'em!"

"Did your Cus say where he bought the *kimono?*" Tom asked the miller.

"No. He did say he was second officer in a trading schooner named *Goodly Miss.* That's all he said. The storm came in and I never had a chance to check on where *Goodly Miss* might be sailing."

"We're headed to Wall. We can ask about her and about Cus Herronsson, if you wish."

"Mama'd be delighted, if they be shipshape and headed home—after this storming. We'd both appreciate hearing news of the boy."

"Consider it done! I know how it is to have no idea where your children have gotten to."

"How will you reach Wall, Librarian? *Oh!* By Dragon—I should have guessed."

"How will we spot it under all this white cover, however?"

"Big notch in the cliff top, of course. Can't miss that! And even covered with deep snow, you'll pick out a fleet of ships laid-to in the roadstead—or tied up at the docks. Ship crews'll clear away ice and snow as quick as they can. The weight alone can snap standing rigging and bring down yards and even masts, y' see."

"I hadn't thought of that. Unless it gets to blowing a lot worse, we'll go on to Wall in the morning and not eat you out of home and mill."

Herron laughed aloud. "Stay as long as you like, Dragons an' all. We'll manage. Plenty of tunny and salmon in yon Peaceful, should meat get short."

Herron's sons and their families arrived, stamping ice from their boots and shedding thick pea –jackets, scarves, mittens, and woolen watch-caps, bearing thickly-frosted chocolate cakes and covered trays of peanut butter cookies, still warm from their own ovens.

"Dinner is ready!" Lily called. "Come and get it b'fore it's all gone!"

Herron was right.

The notch stood out, sharp edges of blue-black granite against snow and clear sky and then bare grey cliffs, falling to where they met the ice-strewn shore and the narrow point of loose stones on which was built the Town of Wall.

And a dozen ships of all sizes and kinds in the anchorage or moored to buoys in the frozen open bay water. As Herron had predicted, all ships had been swept clear of snow and stood out clearly.

Beyond the protectively circling stone walls that framed the inner harbor, was open, unfrozen and uneasy Peaceful Ocean.

"We'll stop at the *Slope*," Manda told Gay and Brenda when they popped their heads from under blankets and furs, blowing clouds of steam. "You remember *Slippery Slope Inn*, Gay? No, you wouldn't—we haven't been here since before you were born."

"I've heard you talk of it, Mama."

"I never even *heard* of Wall." Brenda sighed, feeling quite dim-witted for a moment.

"Everything's *all* so very interesting to learn about, sweetheart! I've never been to your Sprend, either," Gay told her. "Always just flew over and looked down on it. Sprend's so lovely and nice!"

Mollified, the Sprend lass and the little Princess clung to the nearest of Retruance's ears and shrieked happily in pretended fear when the Dragon trimmed his wings and plunged to the inn yard below.

"You burn sea coal? Rather pricey, I would think," Manda said to Mistress Squiller, the Innkeeper's wife.

"Far cheaper and better than buying hardwood brought by wagons or sledges from the inland forests," Flavia Squiller explained, tucking-in another blanket.

They were on the floor above the busy Common Room. Tom had gone at once to the frosted front windows. He scrubbed the thick coating of icy tracery from the windowpanes and began examining the ships he could see along shore and in the harbor with a sailor's glass.

"Lots of Gantrell bottoms," he said aloud. "I recognize them by their flags, even with their sails furled."

"Gantrell sails carry huge pictures of lions," Gay said, to show off. "Or is it a leopard?"

"*I* saw a leopard at your house," Brenda said, trying to keep up with her friend. "Big, long, sharp teeth!"

" No, that was a *jigguar.* Julia the Jigguar."

"She told me she was a leopard, Gay!"

"Julia is a great tease," Tom insisted. "So is Gay! Say you're sorry, Gay!"

"She *does* like to tease me so! I've forgotten it. Let's go explore this inn, Gay. It's ten times bigger and fancier than our *The Babbling Bass* in Sprend."

"Stay indoors where it's warm and safe," Manda called after them. "Wall has some pretty naughty people…"

"I'll be a dutiful Papa and keep an eye on 'em," Tom promised.

He closed the spyglass, slid it into his coat pocket, and went after the girls.

The windows had already frosted over again.

"Getting too dark outside to see, anyway," Tom thought, starting down the wide main stairs.

"I'd say this here storm is—*unusual,* at best," a wind-burnt sailorman at the bar told Tom. "Not in my memory, at least. I ran off to sea at ten. Served on old *Principal.* Out of Wall she was; fifty year ago! Captain was— what *was* his name? *Smith,* I believe…"

Tom listened politely, sipping slowly at a stein of ale.

"There's a vasty green beast at the back door, asking for you, Sir Tom," said the barkeep called Anthony.

Tom went to the door and all eyes in the warm, booze-y Common followed him.

"Evening everybody! Tom!" Retruance—or the small part of him that showed through the doorway, greeted them all. "Word from Flo! He says he'll be here by morning."

"Nobody knows the Everfrost better—unless it's the Ice Dragon. Has *anybody* heard from Hoarling, yet?"

"No, Companion. But you know independent old Hoarling. He'll answer when it suits *him,* not you nor me."

"Where have you guys found to roost?"

"Hetabelle and her kits went off to a cavern just up the cliff half way. I am here and the boy Brazier is circling above, reporting every hour or so. Too many Dragons flitting about make sailors nervous."

He chuckled at the thought. "But we're all on call, as needed."

"Let me know as soon as Flo appears, please. Not much more we can do tonight. C'mon, Blackly. We'll take a look outside till the cold drives us back inside."

He turned to find Gay and Brenda, but they were nowhere to be seen.

"Last call came while you were talking in the Dragon's ear," Anthony the Barman told him.

"Where did my daughter and her maid get to?"

"Headed up to bed. It's later than you think, Sir Tom. Almost midnight!"

Tom realized how weary he was as he trudged up the stair.

"Where's Brenda, my dear?" his night-gowned wife asked as he began to undress.

"Isn't she with Gay?"

"She was—then said she was going back down to fetch her sweater. I let her go, knowing you were there."

Tom swore an unappreciative oath all fathers sometimes used—but silently—pulling his on shirt again. He went back down to Common Room, now empty except for Flavia Squiller and her night crew, mopping floors, wiping tables, and collecting dirty mugs, steins, glasses, bowls and plates.

"Haven't seen the little lassie, Sir Tom," Flavia said.

She called loudly, "Anybody seen the little Sprend maiden around and about?"

Nobody had, even after looking under tables, behind the bar and in the conveniences, out back.

"Had to close the front door, just now," admitted a boy with a long handled broom. "Usually, sir, Master closes and locks it at call of 'Time.'"

"Maybe the lassie went out for a breath. Not that I'd blame her much," Tom said. "Awfully funky in here this time of night!"

"Worse and ever more worrying!" Flavia gasped. "Everybody! Stop what you're doing and help us find the child."

"You and you—follow me," the Librarian called. "Fetch torches!"

Two hours later, Tom had to admit the little girl had simply disappeared. Not a trace of her anywhere around *Slippery Slope's* buildings, barns, stables, storage sheds, or yards.

But on the street a hundred steps from the inn's front door, the boy with the long pushbroom found a red wool sweater with a small golden Dragon embroidered upon its left breast.

CHAPTER TEN
Searching for Brenda

"I'm so sorry! So *sorry!* I should *never* have let her go down alone. Not at midnight!" Manda wailed. "Oh, Tom! What can we do? What will we say to Brenda's mother? How will we explain it to Gay?"

"Squiller has organized a search party; already out. A hundred men on the streets by now, looking. We'll find the lass, darling."

"I need to do more than sit and weep," Manda said, fiercely wiping her eyes. "Is it light, yet? I want to help search..."

"Come along, then. Dress warm! Daylight is still three hours away, but everybody has brought torches and lanterns."

Tom turned to lead her down the stairs, then stopped half-way down.

"Where's the Ramhold dog?"

"Out to the stables, I think." Manda pushed back her fur-trimmed hood. "He said it was much too hot upstairs and..."

"I remember. Also I remember stories of shepherd's dogs who found children lost out on the open plains, miles from anywhere!"

"I—I—remember!"

"Go and find Squiller and his goodwife by the front door. I want that dog with us!"

He disappeared under the stair toward the back door that opened on the Yard. Sensing the unrest and uproar inside the Common, the horses and ponies were astir, asking questions, snorting and stamping their hooves.

"Who has seen a dog—Blackly, a Ramhold sheep dog?" Tom asked several times. At last a bay mare nodded toward a pile of hay spilled down from the loft above.

"He's slept there all evening. I wish *I* could sleep like that!"

"Blackly, old puppy! "Tom called. "Come! Work to be done, boy! Here!"

The strawstack stirred and a black nose poked out; then black eyes blinked sleepily.

"How? Who?"

"We need your expert help, Blackly! Brenda has gone missing."

By the time the dog had wriggled out from under the straw and shaken himself, he realized how important this job was. True to his breed, he was eager to begin at once.

"Where was she last seen? Did she go alone? What was she wearing? A bunch, I bet, in this cold! Prob'ly one of those nice, smelly, thick, sheepskin coats made from one of Ramhold's finest. *Ah!* I smell 'er! Here at the front door…"

He stood on the doorstep and took three deep breaths, testing the temperature, the odors in the cold air, and the time of night."

"We *think* she was alone," Tom told him, "and she was not dressed for outside, we believe. One of the boys found her sweater, over here."

"Yes! Yes! I get it. But she went beyond where the sweater was found."

He started down a narrow, dark side alley away from the inn.

"And…she was *not* alone, Tom! Let me check. Nobody I ever smelt, before. Youngish man-elf, I'd say. Had plums and cream after roast lamb his last meal…which he ate here at our inn, on the sideboard. Brenda had… *um!*— salami and rye. That's very good! Make her hard to miss. How old was the lass?"

"About eight years. Will you lead the way?"

"In this town I'd say we could use some help. A trusted bowmen behind us. I think this man-elf is not any resident of Wall."

"How can you tell?" Manda asked as the dog moved eagerly down the dark alley.

"He smells of saltwater soap and deep-sea sailor's sweat. And he's never skinned a squirrel nor sat close to a pinewood fire in a forest. A sailor in our midst, I say. Come on! Less talk, please."

The way he followed dropped down to the far western end of the docks and ended abruptly at a boat landing Tom recognized from an earlier visit.

"No boatmen here, this night," he groaned. "Where do they go when not working their trade, I wonder."

Squiller, who'd joined the dog's followers at a point higher in Wall, pointed to a row of one-storey stone huts nearby. "Most of 'em live right here."

Tom sent him to the nearest house to rouse the family living there, and shortly an elderly man with a white beard and a sailor's pea jacket and watch cap pulled down over his ears, came out and greeted the Innkeeper and, recognizing Manda and Tom, came over to salute them by touching his cap.

"O' course, Librarian. Recognize you and your lady! Me boys and I helped you rescue the mother and her brood held prisoners on a Gantrell square-rigger."

Tom explained the urgency of their search and the boatman studied the wharf edge and the oaken bollards sticking out of the ice below.

"No boat missing I can see, sir. We gave up working in the inner harbor five, six hour ago. Not worth the risks, what with the awful visibility—and nobody wanted to hire us, anyway."

"But the scents of the girl-child and her captor ends here, you see," Blackly insisted. "Is the ice thick enough to walk upon? I could follow their spore further. Perhaps."

"Saw young Tentrey break through last evening when he tried to walk on the ice. It keeps breaking up and re-freezing. Very dangerous for a grown man—and you look like you weigh-in at nearly as much," said the boatman.

Blackly studied the ice and shook his head. "I don't mind swimming in cold water but where would the damned kidnapper go? No other small boats were moored here."

"Well," said the boatman, "There are signs, here and here, *something* was tied off here during the night. The question is: not where they tied up, you see, but where they coulda gone when they came back and claimed their skiff?"

"I see your point," Tom said. "Unless he went out to one of the ships out in clear water. We'll have to go look, then, Blackly. Can you help us once again, Boats?"

"For you, Librarian, I'll get the boys out of bed and we'll have to chip a couple of our skiffs from the ice. Take an hour or two, I 'spect."

"Squiller, keep your volunteers looking—in case the baby-snatcher took her elsewhere in Wall in his boat. Blackly and I'll check the ships in the roadstead as soon as possible."

"I'll s-s-stay, too." Manda shivered. "Tell us about these ships, Master Boatman, please. Who owns them and who commands. It may help us choose who to approach first."

"Good thinking, Princess. *Whoa!* Dragons!"

The first faint light of dawn over the cliffs caught the glimmer of the wings of Retruance and Brazier Constable. From somewhere in the dark, folded face of the cliffs rose a line of somewhat smaller wings; Hetabelle and her Dragonettes.

Tom said into the sudden dockside silence, "Look off seaward!"

Beyond the end of the stone mall and the moored ships in the open roadstead, a great plume of white water shot into the air. More than two miles offshore, it's roar was deafening. At the peak of the fountain flew a startlingly green-blue Dragon bigger even than Retruance.

"It's the Sea Dragon of Pelehoehoe Island!" Manda cried. "Come ashore, Flo. All you beautiful Dragons will make quick work of finding poor Brenda."

By midday, with the help of seven Dragons and a hundred searchers from Wall, all twelve merchant ships anchored in the roadstead and nearly twenty others moored in the ice or docked at the wharves had been examined.

"No sign of captor or the child," sighed Retruance, returning to report at *Slippery Slope Inn.* "The trail Blackly followed to the Hard is all we can find, hear, or see. He escaped to sea, somehow."

"I'm sure nobody passed overhead or up the pathway, heading inland," Hetabelle said.

"And I would have seen anything in the open sea in my direction," the Sea Dragon said. "I saw three pods of whales, well to the southwest, and a huge school of tuna and another of mackerel. Two walrus families migrating south. No birds of any size in that direction, either."

"If we but knew what kind of ship the kidnapper had," Tom mused aloud, "we'd know what it was capable of doing."

The bone-weary Squiller couple and their people managed to feed and serve hot coffee to the *posse* of men, women, children, eight Dragons and one dog at noon.

"We'll look all over again," the Innkeeper promised Tom. "Soon as everybody has had a bite to eat. Maybe a nap."

"If they wish to go on looking," the Librarian agreed, himself almost asleep over a sandwich. Even the strongest seaman's coffee mess was not keeping him alert and awake. Manda slept beside him, holding a very serious-looking Gay on her lap.

"You did your best," Hetabelle soothed the sad Blackly, almost too tired even to tackle the roast beef Flavia had laid before him.

"From here, I think we Dragons can follow the trail. With lunch aboard, I'll lead them all, along with Flo, to the northwest. Somewhere out there is a ship or boat of *some* kind to catch."

"Take me along," Blackly insisted, perking up his ears. "I can still catch a scent on a sea breeze, even never having been to sea, before."

"If you can," Retruance agreed. "Will you go with us, Companion?"

"Tom and I *and* Gay," Manda said without opening her eyes. "We can catch up on our sleep once a-wing."

"One good-smelling hound, two Princesses, and a Librarian—should be enough," Retruance considered. "One Dragon to stay behind. *Just in case.*"

"If Papa Arbitrance were here…" began his sister-in-law.

"Arbitrance is with his Companion and Murdan is with the King. Both are needed to provide the King wisdom and some reliable, fast transportation," Tom explained. "Furbie must stay with Clem and his family, for now. Flo is sure the Tiki can offer us some good advice about the…*beings*… who stirred the storm."

"Speaking of which," Blackly put in, "does anyone notice? The storm is over and today is considerably warmer than the last week or ten days."

"Thank goodness, it's true!" Manda yawned. "And here I was thinking I was coming down with a fever! Let's shed some of these clothes and climb back on your Dragon, Tom."

"My wife, the Warrior Princess!" Tom chuckled. "We can be ready in a quarter hour, Retruance. I suggest you scaled beasts use the time to decide who of you will stay here as rear guard."

"It'll have to be either Brazier or Bravura."

"I've got more experience than *she* does," the male twin insisted.

"How does a poor Dragonette gain experiences if nobody ever lets her?" His twin sister snorted a jet of angry orange flame.

"She's not had a fair share of important duties," Hetabelle admitted. "Brass Nose and all that, she shall go with us. Brazier, you stay in Wall. Help them melt off streets and wharves and rooftops."

"*Aw,* Mama!" Brazier squeaked, but stern frowns from mother and uncle warned him to be quiet.

"Goody!" Bravura giggled. "I'm ready to go!"

❧ ❧

"One more Dragon to contact," the sleepy Librarian said once they were aloft.

"I 'spect Hoarling will soon show his usual sneer," Retruance sighed, "now we're headed his way."

"Princess Mother?"

"Yes, my darling Princess Daughter?"

"Will we find my best friend Brenda? I fear for her!"

"So do we, precious. So do we! We will certainly try...*very* hard."

"You and Daddy and me! I feel it, down deep. Poor Brenda...I only hope she's as comfortable as we are, Mama."

CHAPTER ELEVEN
Storm Passages

Brenda spent the first hours of captivity in abject terror, expecting to die at any minute. Her captor had gagged her with his own wool kerchief and tied her ankles and wrists with bits of line...not *too* tight but not comfortable, at all, for a child used to running free.

Where that awful little man carried her she never could say. She remembered only darkness, ice and snow and bitterest cold. When she began shivering uncontrollably, he snatched an empty potato sack from a pile of trash and wrapped it around them both.

He said not a word.

When she came to her senses at last, she found she was laid on a smelly, lumpy, old mattress in a bare, wooden bunk. The state of her mind and stomach, it seemed at first, made the room pitch, yaw and roll.

She decided at last she was aboard a ship. She'd never been aboard anything larger than a rowing boat on the river at Sprend, so peacefully and blue-green in summertime.

She took a deep and ragged breath, held it as long as she could, and managed somehow to stop weeping. Some inner sense told her to explore, as much as she could, these fearsome surroundings.

She found she was no longer trussed like a hog, but the tiny cabin in which she found herself, as far as she could tell, seemed locked fast. She heard footsteps overhead and an occasional hoarse shout. No matter how carefully she listened, she could not understand what was said—something to do with the workings of the ship, she decided,

For it *was* a ship. She heard the shrill creakings and loud groaning of ropes and timbers.

As the darkness deepened into night, she smelled cooking and suddenly realized how terribly hungry she was. Were these monsters going to starve her to death?

Shortly, however, the door was yanked open and a young man, merely a boy really, entered carrying an earthenware bowl and a wooden spoon.

"Supper!" the lad announced.

"Who are y-y-you, sir?"

"Never you mind, Princess. Eat—or I'll eat it for you. Rations be short for us, too."

"Where...where are you taking me?" Brenda asked, reaching for the dirty spoon. "What is this stew, pray?"

The ship's boy shook his tangled mop of yellow-grey hair and shrugged. "Rations. Gods alone know what that cook puts in. Just eat it, Princess—or it's mine!"

Brenda ate the hot portion of the slumgullion, ignoring the slimy, greasy liquid and the slivers of—whatever it was.

"Some sort of...meat?" she asked.

Ship's boy shook his head but refused to answer.

She ate quickly and pushed the bowl away, swallowing hard to keep from gagging. The boy snatched the spoon from her hand, took up the bowl and left without further conversation.

Whatever her supper had been, it finally stayed down and she felt a bit better.

There was a loud rattle of rigging, a rush of bare feet and shouted orders—Brenda *presumed* they were orders; she didn't understand a word other than an occasional foul word she'd heard in her father's taproom—and the deck under her suddenly righted to level and then tilted the other way, rumbling like a beast of some insane sort.

Things settled down a bit, finally, as the darkness outside became absolute. Brenda fell asleep on the hard bunk after covering herself against the cold with the now-familiar sacking.

"Flo Sea Dragon has reached Tom at Wall," Furbetrance announced at breakfast. "They're going to follow a ship they think kidnapped poor little Brenda."

Clem put down his second mug of coffee and looked up in surprise. "Brenda? Why Brenda, of all people?"

"What do *we* do, next?" Thomas Clemsson asked.

"I have been considering such for most of the night," Byron Boldface said. "I have compiled as much as I can remember of Northern Hintoo. Not nearly enough, I fear. Our friend Furbetrance has already transmitted it to Flo for Tom. There's nothing more I can do from here."

"What next, Tiki?"

"Go to Hintoo. Research on the ground?"

The Woodsman considered his suggestion for a moment and nodded. "Return to Hintoo with me."

"I will. Not with any great pleasure, perhaps, but—from everything you have told me—it's necessary. And a bit of repayment for rescuing my people from the volcano."

"You and me, aboard Furbie. Only! No Mornie, me sweet wife! Not you nor the boys. Hintoo is dangerous. And I don't have any idea how big a country is Hintoo. One of us gets stranded there, he'd probably *never* get found."

"But..." two sons and a worried wife objected.

"*No!* We can't take the risk. You will stay here and finish my recovering for me. I'll keep you informed by Dragon Telegraph."

"But...!" Mornie wanted to point out that the only available Dragon would be with the men flying to distant Hintoo, not here in Isthmusi.

"I agree," murmured Furbetrance. "I suggest I call one of my kits to come and guard you, Mistress. I understand my young Brazier is unhappy and unemployed, having been left behind at Wall."

"Well, all right then." Mornie sighed dutifully. "I must agree looking for trouble in a far and foreign land might not be best..."

"Truth honestly told," the Tiki said, chuckling to soften his words, "this will be a dangerous mission. A knight and an ancient Tiki will not always have attention to give family. I am truly sorry, Mistress! Hintoo has many beautiful and fascinating places you and your husband—and your sons—would greatly enjoy. Perhaps some time in future?"

Mornie shrugged. The boys looked downhearted, but said nothing.

"I'm ready, then," Clem said. "How long before you'll be available, Byron?"

"After lunch, I should think, Woodsman. I am a light traveler. A few pieces of warmer clothing borrowed from your pack, perhaps."

"Furbetrance Constable?"

"Better the sooner," the Dragon said, puffing out a thin chartreuse cloud. "I wonder, however, if you've any maps or charts to guide us once we reach Hintoo, Tiki, my dear?"

"A few on parchment. Some of them very ancient. An old-man's memory is still good at directions, distances, appearances, people and places, however."

Dragon Telegraph, as Tom had termed it long ago, worked quite well, most days. Some days—or nights—it failed for no apparent reason and for long hours, as it was failing now.

"Most likely electrical storms, somewhere. Or the positions of the moons," Retruance said, climbing high enough to avoid the blustery sea level winds.

"One of those must be causing interference, I suppose. Keep eyes on the flight path ahead *and* to either side," Tom reminded the others, both passengers and Dragons. And the black dog. "She's a small sort of ship, perhaps. And not able to sail straight against the wind. Side to side on tacks, I presume."

"We're all watching, aren't we kits?" called Hetabelle to her brood. "Keep careful station, there, Baby Blue! And let us know when you tire. We can stop for a rest, if needed."

"Yes, Mama!" the youngest Dragon-daughter piped.

"We should catch them up before too very long," Retruance said. "They have to tack, as you say, against this wind?"

Tom nodded. "If I read those wave-patterns, wind's still strong from the northwest, but much easier now than in the past two weeks."

"A new storm is brewing up ahead," Retruance pointed out three hours later. "We may have to sit down somewhere and ride it out, not only because of the wind but because we could easily miss the culprit in a storm."

Tom leaned out over the great Dragon's wide eyebrow, training Murdan's powerful pocket telescope on the heaving sea ahead.

No island, nor reef, nor sandbar to be seen.

And no ship!

Snow began to fall from the leaden skies. Retruance melted it away from his wings, head, neck and back as fast as it settled, but it was a bad choice for his passengers, and Tom asked his Companion to let the stuff pile up. It was better and seemed warmer than melt-water soaking their garments.

"For a very short while," the Dragon said. "But snow has great weight and I must clear it off or we may end up paddling in the Peaceful."

"Do you see any dry refuge, anywhere?" Manda called. "I think it's time to settle down, keep warm, and get fed, husband dear."

Tom nodded but for some time, as the weather grew steadily worse, there was nothing on the sea but great, grey northeast-bound breakers.

Baby Charlie dropped lower and lower as her young pinions wearied.

She pretended it was to see the surface better, but her mother noted her flame was coming, now, in frosty white puffs—not her usual pale blue.

Hetabelle opened her mouth to ask for a rest stop—but she was anticipated by her eldest Dragon-daughter, off to her side.

"Mama! Master Tom! Mistress Manda! Gay! Sea Dragon! Blackly! An island! Ahead and down to the right just a bit!"

"We have no choice," Hetabelle called to Tom. "Although I know I could carry Baby on my back for some hundreds of miles, yet."

"No, no; we *all* need a break from this. Everybody? Follow Bravura down!"

Retruance snapped his wings in agreement, calling, "Land in a sheltered spot if you can, Brass Nose! I'll scout a better place after every body is on solid grounding, out of this half-gale."

Needle-sharp pinnacles of stone rushed up at the Line of Flight following the plummeting Brass Nose, who marked the way through the grey gloom of swirling sleet and fog with a continuous plume of orange flame.

The Dragonette swiveled right, then slid left, then spun about, screaming in a most unladylike fashion as she braked to a full stop to avoid smashing into a wall and, winging over, dropped like a huge lavender blossom into a cleft between two rock faces.

"Down!" she cried. "Come on down! Plenty of room and no wind, here."

"Good girl!" Retruance grunted as he touched down softly in a snow-bank. "Everybody okay?"

"Broke a fore-claw, dammit!" Hetabelle snarled.

"Mama!" gasped Gorgonzola, who had managed to make a fairly graceful four-point landing in a thick clump of ground pine. "Such language!"

"Watch your tongue!" her mother snapped.

"Are you well, Gay?" Manda asked. "A bit of a bump, Tom?"

"Fine as pink satin, Mama! *What fun!*" Gay squealed in delight.

"I came in last and much slower," Flo explained to Tom, crossing his wings overhead to protect the canyon floor from the falling snow. "Your eldest daughter is a bit—over enthusiastic, Mistress Hetabelle."

"Get me killed, one of these days," Hetabelle agreed, but she smiled. "You're forgiven, Brass Nose, dear. Mama is just getting too old for aerial acrobatics."

Bravura—Brass Nose—seemed about to argue the point, but gave her mother a warm hug, instead.

Peace was restored. Pains disappeared shortly thereafter.

After checking to see that everybody was safely under cover, Tom, Blackly and Retruance explored higher up the crevasse, lighted by a steady yellow blaze provided by the Dragon.

At the far upper end the sides closed in overhead, making it a tall narrow cave.

"Plenty of nice dry space here," Blackly pointed out after a quick sniff around. "Move everybody up and let's have a nice hot supper. This storm should blow over by morning, I guess."

The Librarian nodded agreement and the oddly-mixed three went to bring the others up into the cavern.

With a steaming roast of beef and baked potatoes and even a bit of carrot salad (a Dragon favorite) from Retruance's storage pouches, and with family Constable and the Sea Dragon giving off excess heat, the cave quickly became quite cozy.

"A special treat for us all!" announced Hetabelle when they'd finished their supper. "I left it outside to freeze. It should be solid by now. Go fetch it, Charlie, dear. It's to celebrate your first important grown-up adventure."

Chartreuse skipped off into the dark outside, through the lighter snow falling now, and returned in less than a minute with a five-gallon metal canister, which contained, when she tore off the cover, strawberry ice cream!

"Who would ever travel without Dragons?" laughed Princess Gay. "Plenty of storage places for the best kinds of food!"

CHAPTER TWELVE
Confusions

Gay awoke early, as usual and, after struggling free of a linen sheet, a heavy wool blanket and a beaver-skin coverlet, skipped to the fire now burning low in the center of the cave.

Everyone seemed deep in sleep. The cave air was pleasantly warmed, both by Dragons and by burning pine. The practical Princess added new sticks and chips to the blaze and waited for it to crackle and surge back to bright life.

"Need more wood," she murmured to the Ramhold herd-dog. "A good job for us, Blackly. Come along!"

"Not too far." Blackly yawned, following the girl toward the cavern entrance. "It's still mighty cold outside!"

"Not *too* bad, however. Here's some firewood! Aunty Hetabelle had the Dragonettes gather it late last night. *Oooff!*"

She carefully selected and hoisted several two-foot split logs on the dog's strong back and, steadying the load with her hands, looked about for something to tie it in place

A sudden raspy male voice startled them!

"*Stand! Make not one false move, me pretty!* Down, you damned cur dog! This here bow is bent at ye!"

Blackly yelped in surprise and growled as fiercely as he could manage in the next half breath. He moved between the girl and the intruder—*intruders,* he saw. These were a dirty, ragged half-dozen bearded men crowding into the entrance to Tall Cave.

"I am Princess Gale Trusslo Whitehead of Carolna and Hidden Canyon," Gay said loudly and carefully, as she had long ago been taught. "And I *give* orders, not *take* them! At least not from such people as you!"

The leader of the invading band of—it appeared—sailors brandishing heavy belaying pins and a few fearsome-edged weapons, was startled by her defiance, but managed to snarl, "Princess or scullery maid, little girl, I want you to fall to the deck and me mates'll bind you up—if you blamed idiots can find some small stuff for the task!"

"I say to you, all six; put down your nasty things and be welcomed inside. It is warmer and we'll have breakfast in a few moments, I promise."

The seamen muttered hungrily and began to talk, all at once.

"Silence!" their leader ordered shrilly. "*I* am your elected Captain, here, am I not?"

"But, Sir Capt'n, sir! We are here offered food and warmth! We're tired and cold and starving!"

"Hush, ye filthy mud-turtles! We'll tie up the maiden and hold her for good rations from her folks. Don't ye see?"

Blackly grinned wickedly around bared teeth, snorting angrily.

"Move one jot or a single tittle and I'll rip you to shreds..."

"You can't stop all six!" shouted the Captain.

"I will need some help, perhaps," the sheepdog admitted.

He glanced upward.

"I have often wondered what fricasseed fool would taste like," came the voice of Retruance Constable from the overhead gloom. "Drop the belaying pins and the knives! File ahead of us toward the fire. Oatmeal with brown sugar and cream, I suspect, will be your punishment for attempted capture of a Princess!"

Tom emerged from his bedroll to find six very frightened seamen kneeling before him. They looked thoroughly sick and hungry, and cowed when Retruance was joined by Hetabelle and her daughters, all breathing wisps of greenish fire and smoke.

And his daughter and Blackly looking pleased as punch.

"How now? Pirates, are you?"

"No, no, no, revered sir! We are simple seamen, formerly in the service of a Wall sea-captain."

"Who's this Captain, then," Tom asked, reaching over to wake his wife.

"I know most of them by name."

" 'Twas old Captain Giller, sir! Him as was lost when *Rollabout Lioness* broke amidships and most drownded, at once."

"But you men survived? Or—did you set your officers adrift in the storm? The bare truth, I demand. I don't trust your looks!"

"Oh, let 'em have some breakfast and then we'll talk," Manda said with a yawn. "They look pretty badly off, I'd say. Frostbite and such?"

"Yes, yes, m'lady! Oh, yes!" the six seamen wailed, bobbing and lifting their hands beseeching mercy. "We ain't had but lichens and a couple sea birds in four days."

Tom nodded but insisted on searching the newcomers personally for hidden weapons—he knew sailors from experience; there's almost always a stray clasp knife or a knuckle-duster hidden somewhere—while Manda set about preparing scrambled eggs and ham bits, served with fried bread and orange marmalade.

And lots of piping hot coffee, best of all.

The disarmed and ravenous sailors and their captors ate and shortly began to talk.

"We was at a small Hintoo seaport called—what was it? Toomani, it were! Captain Giller..."

"When was this?" Retruance interrupted.

"Hard to say, Sir Dragon! Terrible blizzard had swept across the coast three, four days afore. Them yellow Hintoos made us nervous. Like *we* caused the blow? Buried their town under two fathoms of snow, I heard."

"Go ahead, then. What did your Captain decide?"

Despite the Carolnans' first suspicions of the battered crewmen, it became obvious to Tom early on they were not connected in any way with the mysterious sloop, which had run off with Brenda.

They had been ordered to leave Hintoo as soon as the high winds died away, the elected new Captain, explained.

Sailing was rough, the winds still blustery and the seas high, he said with a convincing shudder. "Captain Griller was not a young man but years of experience gave him tools to save his ship and men. There were things we'd ordinarily have done, afore we left port for the Peaceful crossing, but they never did—*could*—get done. Weather was too harsh! Worth a man's life to claw into the tops. We lost four, trying their best. Ol' Capt'n called the rest of us off."

The wind, rough and wild, was fair for Wall, so they went running before it with bare poles until the night of the third day out.

"I was grabbing a bit of sleep by the galley stove at last and woke to cries of dismay and fear, you can believe me, Sir Thomas! I don't know if the helmsman was asleep or if the lookouts couldn't see—although the night was clear. There came a terrible, terrible grinding and sounds of timbers smashing and rigging snapping...and I found meself in water black as hard coal!"

"I was on deck when it happened," another seaman added. "We didn't see the rocks until way too late. Ship ran broadside onto one, faster'n a man could think."

"Figure p-p-poor *Lioness* s-s-snapped right in two!" sobbed a third hand, trembling like a willow leaf. "Figure the only of us escaped were them on deck when she hit. Us five, is all. Captain, officers, ten crewmen asleep in the fo'castle—all gone in a trice! We never found a s-s-single body on shore."

Manda made a soft, sympathetic gasp and handed the weeper another cup of coffee.

"I'm ship's carpenter," explained the new Captain. "I had flint and steel on me. Started a fire of driftwood we found ashore. A signal for them still in the water—and keep us from freezing..."

"I'm so sorry! I forgot to ask your name," Tom interrupted again.

"I be Cus, Sir Knight. Narcissus, actually. Crew calls me Chips."

"By the Gods!" cried both Tom and Manda as one. "You're brother to our very best friend, Clematis Herronsson!"

"Ye know ol' Clem! What a marvel! This sort of thing *never* happens, gentle people! In all the wide Peaceful..."

Manda flung her arms around the man's neck, laughing in pure delight. Tom shook his hand and then thumped him on his sturdy back.

"I *thought* you looked familiar," Retruance grinned. "But—Clem and his family spoke of their youngest as a ship's officer!"

"I'm sorry to say I lead them all to believe I was of higher rank." The youngest Herronsson blushed. "It was why I never went home, much. Until I got a better rank and larger pay."

"Well, you're welcome as can be," Tom assured him. "And Retruance here can tell Clem we've found you, right away. There's no way to tell your parents and siblings just now. They'll be delighted to hear you're safe and sound."

"Some doubt about the *safe* part," Cus said. "We're still cast up on this cold and rocky place. And likely to be here a long while. This island has no trees—not even enough to make a hut for shelter, let alone a canoe or a boat!"

"We'll set you safe to home, never fear," Manda assured him and his mates. "Plenty of head-room. Enough for all!"

Tom shook his head. "If time was right! We have a very important task first. In fact, *two* jobs. We must rescue a little girl from pirates—*and* we have been charged by our liege to trace these arctic storms—if they are natural or magical."

"My crew agrees," said Cus. "We will cast in with you. Pirates can be *very* bad men! Deadly! Can we be a help?"

"I! It isn't a matter of numbers…"

"It's the least we can do," Cus insisted. "Honor you for saving us— honor dead Capt'n Griller and our drowned crewmates, too."

"I am afraid not, Cus. If I could, I would send you home, for your mother's sake, alone. The young Dragon'll ferry you to the Hintoo coast. We'll give you weapons to defend yourselves, and some warm clothing. And return to pick you up when our tasks are finished."

In the end, the shipwrecked crewmen reluctantly agreed.

Over lunch Tom sorted out his plan to find and free Brenda.

"There's a risk the storm-makers, whoever they are, will move against Carolna, as we were warned. But the little girl needs us even worse."

"I agree!" his wife said. "Carolna—my father and my uncle and men like Ffallmar—can hold their own without us, I 'spect. For a while, at least."

Tom stood, stretched, and said, "We will go on looking for Brenda's captors. Cus, we've assigned your people to the Dragonettes. They'll find you a perch of safety—and provender and water and shelter. Then the Dragonettes will return to us. We'll see you within a fortnight, I'd say."

"I understand," was all Cus could say. "We'll wait you out, Librarian!"

"Take-off in fifteen minutes. Twenty at the most. Anything you have to take care of—do it now!" said Retruance loudly for all to hear.

Nobody felt badly about leaving the rocky isle behind.

CHAPTER THIRTEEN
Hintoo Welcome

Furbetrance glared at the heavily-armed platoon of soldiers escorting Clem and the Tiki out to his roosting in an orange grove just beyond the city gate.

"Here less than four hours." He snorted a jet of pale blue sarcastic smoke at the archers, who came to an abrupt halt. "...and in trouble, already?"

"Not so!" Byron smiled, bowing respectfully to the Dragon. "Our friends here in Chang Wallow are providing us an Honor Guard, only. Also to make sure we don't stay beyond our welcome, too, I admit."

"This is Captain Wrong Pu," Clem said. "Captain, this is the Dragon, Furbetrance Constable of whom we have been speaking to your master."

The officer in red lacquer breastplate and tall feathered helmet bowed even more deeply than had the Tiki.

"I am most sorry, sir! Our Lord Mandarin has ordered us to see you on your way. Please do not give us any problem about it. We are authorized to use deadly force to carry out his orders!"

"I also am sorry," Clem said, shaking his head. "We will leave at once. May we ask..."

"How you plan to combat a Constable Dragon?" Furbetrance snorted angrily. "We came in peace, seeking information..."

"I don't know details, Fearsome Monster!" the officer said, stepping back hastily to avoid Furbie's fiery breath. "I am just following orders!"

"Easy!" Byron warned the Dragon. "We talked to his Supreme Mandarin and the locals have good reason. They have great fears of us—especially Dragons."

"We stand little chance to get help here," the Woodsman grumbled. "Not by favor nor by force!"

"Still..." rumbled the Dragon. "It might be worth a try!"

Clem climbed to Furbie's left knee, but paused there.

"A question or two, if I may, Captain Wrong?"

The captain nodded.

"How's the weather been here this winter so far?"

Wrong considered, then answered, "Colder than usual. Windy. A lot of rain and even some snow! Not usual, Sir Woodsman."

"And one more: have you heard of much more—*uh*—severe weather elsewhere?"

"One always hears such things." The soldier shrugged. "Now, please, Woodsman! Depart our principality before I must use force!"

"Wind's out of the northwest, perhaps?" Retruance asked, mildly.

"From the north-by-northwest, Fearsome Beast. Farewell!"

The blue-and-silver Dragon shot into the cloudy sky and circled to the west. The red-armored soldiers trotted back toward their walled city, sighing in relief.

A tall figure, wrapped in three wool scarves, a thick sailor's sweater over his breastplate and another beneath and a knitted bonnet under his steel helmet, reined his enormous plow-horse to a weary stand before Alix Amanda Palace in Lexor.

"Ffallmar o' Ffallmar Farm," the badly iced and snow-dusted knight announced to a startled guard. "I am called before the King."

"Yessir! *Yessir!* He's been asking of you, Sir Ffallmar. He's here, now. Please step down and follow me."

A liveried courtier stopped them outside the Royal Suite.

"His Majesty is *not* to be disturbed! Leave your name and wait, like all the rest of them below."

"Damned fool!" hissed the guardsman. "This is Ffallmar of Ffallmar Farm. His Majesty has been waiting to see him these three, four days. Announce him!"

The double door banged so wide the heavy oaken leaves boomed at the golden stops like bass drums. Ffallmar was still stripping off his wet winter clothing and stamping ice from his boots when Eduard and Murdan rushed from an inner room.

"*Now* we can get some things done," the King greeted his Knight Commander. "Come in by the fire."

"Is the weather any better, to the west?" Murdan asked anxiously. "Is the snow melting?"

"Better—but freezing again at night, Historian. *Ah!* Hello, Altruance!"

"I brought the Historian from Overhall, actually. Good to see you, Ffallmar. What can we do for *you?*"

"I would surely welcome something hot to drink, if you could."

Settled before the royal fire with a bucket of tea, Ffallmar drank and sighed deeply and said, "I am here to serve, Lord King."

"We neglected to ask about my Rosemary and your family, Son. Forgive me!" Murdan interrupted.

"Everybody was snow-bound, well fed and warm as toast when I left." the farmer-soldier said. "What's the situation here, Sire?"

"Tell him what he must know, Murdan. Then we can talk and order things done, being better informed."

The Historian took less than an hour to lay before the Knight Commander all that had been said, done, guessed, learned and feared about the storm.

"We hope to get more from Tom and Clem and the Tiki, very soon. Tom and his Dragons are chasing the kidnapper on the high sea, as I said..."

"But you have no further word about the storms, is that it?"

The Historian shrugged and nodded.

"Any Wizards or Magi we can get to help?"

Eduard told him, "Walden—my Lord Chamberlain—says most of them, like Arcolas, went somewhere south to a conventicle."

"Let me sit back a moment and think about this." Ffallmar sighed. "I've been in the saddle two days and nights. I'm tired and hungry and wet to the skin."

"Of course! But does anything suggest itself to you, Ffallmar? We're near to distraction, ourselves."

"See if you can get word to them fool Wizards. Send soldiers and citizens out to open main roads for traffic. Does anybody know how to predict weather, at all?

"I usually am very good at it," Murdan said. "But I missed these storms altogether!"

"Father-in-Law, you are an amateur prognosticator, I know, but we need a *professional*. Sea Captains and fishermen depend on such, I've heard!"

"I'll find 'em. Bring them hither," the King promised. "You've at least given us somewhat to do. Sleep for a while. I'll have breakfast or lunch or dinner brought when you awake."

"Not much sense doing just...*something*," Ffallmar muttered sleepily. "Not good generaling to rush off not knowing what you're about—or why!"

He was deeply asleep before the brothers left the room and the Dragon left the window.

CHAPTER FOURTEEN
The 'Princess' and the Pirates

Dragons—especially Sea Dragons—have a remarkable sense of direction. They can find their way anywhere despite twirling, swirling buffets of wind, waves, cold rain and low hard-edged grey clouds.

"The problem is," Retruance Constable said to Flo, "I know *we're* going right, but I don't know how wrong these pirate people have gone. They could be heading in nine different directions, all away from our line!"

Flo nodded thoughtfully but didn't answer. He'd caught an interested ogle from starboard, shot his way by Bravura Constable!

"Retruance?" he asked softly. "I seem to have—unwittingly, I assure you!—attracted the—*attention? adoration? worship?*... of your pretty pink niece, over there. How should I react? A lonely life at sea doesn't prepare one for such attention."

The other Dragon chuckled, producing a flight of orange perfumed smoke rings. "You haven't much experience with females, do you? Well," he added more seriously, "the pink lassie has a keen eye for you, Flo, and all I can say is she has good taste. I congratulate you, sir."

"I am relieved. I was afraid her mother and father, your brother, might...object!"

"*Never* object! If you pinned us down, we all three would admit we're pleased; even flattered."

"I will second the motion," called Hetabelle, who was near enough to hear the conversation. "No rush, however. Let it develop naturally. As I can attest, good mates and lovers are hard to find among us Dragons."

She drifted a bit closer, to lower her voice.

" 'Til right now, my dear Florenz, the only possible marriage match for our little girl was that nasty Hoarling Frostbite. I have had nightmares of welcoming him into the family!"

"Oh, Hoarling's not nearly as bad as he likes to pretend," said Manda. "But I must agree, I'd rather see my daughter being courted by someone like you, Flo."

The Sea Dragon coughed an embarrassed cloud of green vapor and changed the subject. "What were you saying, Retruance? Something about finding those despicable kidnappers?"

Brenda, at that moment, was *almost* enjoying her captivity.

The wind had moderated and even the land-bred lass could tell the ship's master, a big, smelly man aptly named Downpour was pleased with what progress they earned by constant tacking-and-running over the past few hours.

"Let the Princess on deck," he called to the ship's boy, "Put her to work. *Everybody* works for his biscuits in my ship!"

The boy, whose name was Crippen, unbarred her cabin door and led Brenda onto *Updraft's* main deck—the first glimpse she'd gained of crew, deck, masts, railings, spars, sails, ropes, cables and ratlines—and the heaving sea all about.

"I'm ordered to put you to work, Princess. What do Princesses do, I wonder? Make and mend shirts? Darn socks? Cook, maybe?"

"I can cook up a storm, if need be. But, judging from what you've been feeding me, there's not much to cook!"

"You be too right about that. *Some* crew are talking of drawing lots. Loser goes in the stew pot!"

"You really mean...? How *horrible!*"

"So's starving to death slowly, Princess. It may come to it, soon. Flour is gone. Meal is very low and mostly spoiled. Salt beef hasn't been seen aboard for over a week! I haven't had more than a taste of stewed hardtack—nor have you!—since two days back."

Brenda turned away to hide the sudden sickness his words caused.

How long had it been since she ate? Four or five full days and nights, at least.

"But—how about the sea birds? And I suppose there're fishes in the sea to be caught, Master Crippen?"

"I don't know about fishes," he answered, "and birds stay away too far and fly too fast and high, Princess. I've *tried* shooting 'em. A terrible waste of arrows!"

"Find us some strong string and a fishhook. We'll try our smarts against some halibut or sea trout—or starve trying."

"I can do it. Catch fishes, Princess? We can but try, I guesses."

"And stop calling me 'Princess,' " she called after him.

The young man paused and looked back, startled.

"*Not* a Princess? I was told you were a Princess of the Royal Family of Carolna!"

"No such thing, I swear it! I am Maid-in-Waiting to a Princess, I will admit. My name is Brenda of Sprend. I can be called "Lady Brenda" if you must give me a title."

"Now! Let's see if a poor, hungry ship's lad and a poor, hungry village girl can outsmart some fish—and quickly!"

With the calming of the waters, it seemed, the fish were hungry and gravitated to *Updraft's* hull. Experience promised easy pickings near such a ship shadow, either slops tossed over the side or small, tasty fingerlings sheltering under the sloop's barnacled bottom.

Using stale bread chunks as bait, the fishers tossed hand lines over the lee side and almost at once pulled up a sea trout, fairly hooked.

"Sailors don't eat fish!" complained the tall, skinny cook. "Never! *Never!*"

"Maids from Sprend catch 'em and eat 'em, believe me. Better by far than being butchered and eaten!" Brenda told him with a firm look.

"Ah, well...I s'pose...well, ye're right! I've heard of some poor souls *living* on fishes. Well and good! How to cook these nasty things? Boil 'em or broil 'em or bake 'em?"

Any village or farm lass of less than ten years was already trained in housewife arts, especially cooking. And Brenda had since early childhood been alert and aware of how her mother ran her home, especially the big, bright, warm inn kitchen, the fiery hearth, and the tools of the art.

She put Crippen to work scraping and scaling the trout, removing heads, fins and tails.

"We could set snares with these heads and stuff," he decided. "Bait for some birds."

They found a small canister of bacon-grease, some coarse sea salt and a pepper grinder, and shortly the odor of frying trout wafted across deck and down to the fo'castle and the captain's cabin.

Tin plates were brought and a bit of old bread found and before it was time to reset the sails for a new tack, everyone had been fed.

Complaining bitterly about being fed *fish*—but eating!

"Never ate such rations, afore!" one deck hand cried, swearing in surprise. "Be better yet with some onions or leeks, mayhap, and a bit of wine."

Leaving Fats the Cook to take full credit, praise even from Captain Downspout, Brenda and the boy went back to their fishing lines, adding to the larder as fast as they could pull in new fish.

Eyes sharpened by full tummies, the masthead lookouts shortly hailed, *"Land ho!"* and the crew rushed forward to see the landfall.

"Where in Bloody Blasted Hades are we?" Downspout screamed and, when nobody could even guess, went below to try to find their place on his sketchy charts of the Hintoo coastline.

After a few minutes his crew saw him scramble to the foretop with a long glass tucked under his arm. Those nearest heard him cursing even more than usual.

"By all the Greater Gods! The map's right! A bloody, stinking *mangrove* swamp, far as eye can see. No dry land, at all!"

The Captain ordered longboat and skiff dropped in the now-calm sea and sent armed crews into the silent sea forest. *"You!* Into the longboat, now!" he shouted at poor Crippen. "Pull your share of sweep, boy! Bo'sun! He don't pull his weight, chuck 'im over the side. One less to feed."

"Look for eats, *I* says," ordered Bo'sun, a hard-boiled old seaman with one eye missing and a pair of fingers gone on his right hand. "Call out if ye see anything. Stay close up. Don't get apart in 'ere!"

The Captain watched them disappear among the trees growing from the water.

"Go wash up them dishes, girl!" he yelled, catching sight of Brenda at the rail. "This be no sightseeing tour, dammit!"

She opened her mouth for an angry retort but, instead, ran off to the galley. She found her new friend, skinny Fats, loading a large tray with fish heads, gills, fins and innards.

"For the seabirds, as you said," he explained. "Messy work! Help me finish, drape the nets, just *so,* and you can go wash yourself. You stink like a dead cod, child!"

"I suppose I do." Brenda sighed, shoveling a mushy, boney pile of fish guts onto the tray. "But I have no clothes, clean *or* dirty! I'll smell worse by the minute. *Ugh!*"

"You'll have to settle for cast-off rags, I guess. You set this bird trap, best as you can, and I'll see what can be found in the lucky bag."

"Lucky bag?" But he'd gone off somewhere below deck.

Fish for supper again, but every bit was devoured. Bread was gone, except for the Captain and his three officers—and the galley slaves, Brenda, Fats and a weary Crippen who nibbled as they cooked and served.

The boats had weaved back and forth among the mangroves, finding nothing to report other than thousands of saucy birds above and millions of tiny fish and shrimps in the dark water.

"We can have shrimps and sardines," Fats crooned happily as he fried halibut steaks. "These seamen wont stand for seafood long, can it be helped."

"You think we'll move on elsewhere?" the ship's boy asked. "But where?"

"These little shrimp things are *very* good," Brenda said around a mouthful. "I recall seeing them—only bigger—at the Lord Historian's table."

"Lords eat better than anybody." Fats laughed. "Better than most sailors, but not better than a careful cook. Fry 'em quickly, little Brenda, or they gets tough."

Brenda popped another peeled, pink shrimp in her mouth and chewed happily.

"This batch is done," she declared, scooping two-dozen of the critters from the frying pan. "Ready for the Captain, now. Best if we leave the skins on, I think, Master Fats. Keep 'em hot on their way to the mess."

"Not much for seasoning but salt and pepper," Fats said thoughtfully. "Tell me. How did the Historian eat 'em?"

"I think he dipped them in a hot sauce of some sort. Pepper and onion and garlic and tomatoes, chopped fine together. I didn't ask—or taste."

Fats found a nearly empty bottle of pepper sauce—always popular with sailors—and mixed some with the last of the onion flakes, a generous pinch of garlic powder, some dried red pepper and a bit of stale beer. "To give it a bite of bitterness."

"We won't be here long, I say," Crippen said thoughtfully, munching the last of the stale cracker crumbs. "Ol' Downpour had some place in mind, carrying you off like he did."

"You mean—Captain Downpour doesn't intend to ask ransom for me. For Princess Gay, I mean. He thinks I'm Gay of Hidden Canyon?"

"Far as I know, little Lady. *I* haven't told him you're not his prize princess. He'll blow his skull when he learns!" the boy said.

"It won't be me who talks of it," said the cook. "Bad enough to tell him we're almost out of fixings like lard and beans and salt pork. But I got to do it right now—or it'll be much worse."

CHAPTER FIFTEEN
Paths Do Cross

The ancient stone pagoda was perched on a low hill overlooking stark white plain in all directions. Clem had used their tenting to screen the north wind from the single door and built a small fire to hold back the evening frost while Furbetrance was off scouting.

"Place makes me jumpy," he said to Byron. "I feel like we shouldn't set foot in it, any."

"I am sure nobody will notice." The Tiki smiled. "The holy monks who built it a thousand years ago have long since disappeared. Nobody knows what happened to them, poor souls. They were good at designing buildings and such things. To me, it seems rather restful, Woodsman."

"I—I—I—respect your wisdom and experience, Tiki. I'm glad you're with us!"

Byron nodded silent thanks and stooped to add to the fire a double handful of wheat straw he'd dug from under the snow. Clem pulled aside the canvas over the temple entrance to peer anxiously out.

In a few more minutes it would be full dark and time for supper.

The northerly wind now was weaker and warmer. But the Woodsman's instinct told him it was soon going to snow once more.

A swatch of darker shadow appeared overhead and black wings flapped to full stop. Furbetrance Constable emerged from a great cloud of white crystals, coming about the temple's upturned roofline.

"Bad flying weather, Woodsman! Visibility less than a few yards! *Whoo!* Supper smells good. Good old Tiki cooking again?"

"Come inside just a bit and tell us what you *did* see—if anything."

Byron looked up with a broad smile at the sight of the ice-trimmed Dragon's head filling the doorway. "Pepper soup with a bit of pork! Your favorite, I believe? It'll be ready as soon as it comes to boiling."

"Who would travel without a handy Tiki?" The Dragon gulped down a gallon of scalding hot soup. "Puts the fire back in the belly!"

"You're not telling us a thing!" Clem growled. "Too much happy talk, says I. What did you see here in this country? Of the villages and the people?"

"Well, to tell you the truth, Clem Herronsson, I *already* told you. I saw fifty trillion snowflakes—each of them different, I'm told—but nothing else, and more to come shortly. Visibility zero, as us professional fliers say."

"I would think you would see *some* people," Byron murmured protest. "This is a densely populated area. Wheat and barley and oats and—all sorts of good farmlands. There must be farmers, somewhere!"

"I'm sorry, Tiki! I flew, maybe, a hundred miles out, around and back by a different route. Didn't see a single cottage or even a bit of rising smoke!"

Clem considered for a moment.

"Well, you wouldn't see much smoke, would you? With this wind, I mean. And the houses and barns and such are generally low, not the tall roofs as farmers in Carolna build 'em. And the roads…"

"Are under deep snow. It has been snowing here for a week or ten days." Byron nodded. "And a wise countryman would take all his stock inside and keep to the fireside doing winter chores until spring comes. He will be praying his firewood and his food last until then, bless his soul."

The ancient pagoda was silent except for the soft crackling of the fire, the moaning of the wind, and the soft hiss of new snow falling. Clem and Byron finished the pepper soup and shared a fistful of ship's crackers.

"No use going further west, I say," Clem said finally. "I think we should take a lesson from my past. Go to the ocean and follow the coast northward. Look for rivers large enough for sea-going ships. We should be able to see the flow of large rivers, at least."

"The old manuscripts mention a big river forming the northern boundary of Hintoo," Byron told them. "It is called Diamond River. I know virtually nothing more of it than the name."

"But large enough to follow, at least, and maybe find some natives *above* snow. We certainly won't find roads and natives here," Clem decided. "And we might cross trails with Tom and Manda and Retruance. They're somewhere up that way."

"Warm up and sleep some," the Dragon suggested.

He would have nodded his great blue head in approval if the temple's decorated ceiling had allowed. "Fly east-north-east until we hit the coast."

"Well and good!" yawned the Tiki. "Enjoy a night of warm, dry beds then. How these ancient bones miss the warmth of my southern sands!"

Retruance Constable warped the trailing edges of his great, black wings, slowing their progress until the line of Dragons were making, Tom estimated, less than ten miles per hour.

"What do you think?" he said to Retruance's nearest ear, the one to his immediate right.

"We'll have to put down, soon, don't you agree? My wings, your eyes, and everybody's bottoms are tiring."

"But…where to land?"

"Sea is calm. We can settle on the water, itself, if no place else. But that haze on the horizon speaks to experienced eyes. There's coastline, there. A few more miles will tell the tale, as Grandfather Constable used to say when the day got worn down to…"

"Land, then!" Tom interrupted, "and you can tell me exactly where we are. You're the trail-master, Companion. No charts for this coast at all."

"Well, from the smell—fragrance, I should say—that will be a mangrove slough. Very common along these coasts, I understand. *Ahoy! Everybody!* Follow old Retruance down. Sharp eyes for that sloop at the same time."

"Either we've missed them a-sea in all the snow and fog or they could be a hundred miles up the coast—or down, either," Manda said.

She sounded discouraged and Tom put his arm around her.

"We'll look carefully around," he told her. "Be good to walk solid ground again, though. No criticism implied, Retruance."

"I see the mangroves!" called Gorgonzola. "See? *Big!* Really big trees! Growing up out in the saltwater shallows. And not much dry land anywhere."

"Follow me, all," Retruance called loudly so all the flyers could hear. "You watch for signs of that wretched sloop. *I'll* see if can I find a bit of hummock dry enough for a fire and some supper."

The Royal Historian swore a fiery string of angry oaths when they stepped out of Alix Alone Palace. Wide Royal Plaza was glazed with wet ice, and melt-water ran like broad, shallow rivers down toward the seaport, carrying a vast tonnage of mud, wood—whole trees!—thousands of shakes and shingles.

"It'll pass." Eduard said calmly. "Nothing even a king can do about it! At least it's not snowing. Much warmer, too, I see. Cheer up, Murdan. The streets are being cleared as quickly as can be. Your Dragon has gone off to help melt and burn and tear things to pieces."

Murdan shaded his eyes against a bright haze still making distant sight nearly impossible. Rain fell at a sharp slant across the field of view.

"Take your word for it, then," he sighed. "What does our Commander-in-Chief say? What can we do to help?"

"He is mustering citizens to clear the streets. I'm to organize food distribution from the Government Storehouses. Ffallmar says most of the food is gone from people's larders. We must forestall food riots!"

Murdan shook his head fiercely, causing a shower of fine snow down his neck from his hat.

"*Dammit!* You feed your people, half-brother. I'm going to track down Master Arcolas and the other useless magicians. We still face the possibility of invasion, don't forget! Somebody *must* know where they got to at the wrong time. *Dammit!*"

The King gestured for his horse—coaches and even wagons were useless, and even a good, heavy war steed would have trouble navigating the icy streets.

"Try Moonlight Quarter. Many Magi have homes there, I understand. Take plenty of money, Murdan! They won't work for nothing."

"They'll work free for the common good, by all that's holy. Else I'll run 'em out of Carolna!"

Manda sleepily pushed a thick fleece blanket off her shoulder and remembered, in the nick of time, to catch it before it fluttered off in the Dragon's slipstream.

"What...?"

Tom turned around and grinned at his wife and their daughter. "Furbie has sighted an island off to the left a bit—a *hummock* as he calls it. He's going down to check it closer."

"About time! My legs're still sound asleep. Oh! *Ouch!*"

"Oh, Mama! Get up and stretch a bit," Gay advised with all the certainty of a ten-year-old.

She watched as Hetabelle and her brood swooped down, following Furbetrance, then examining the thickly overgrown islet in the midst of the swamp.

"Island safe and dry," they smoke-signaled to the Sea Dragon, far above.

Flo relayed the message to Retruance and his passengers. "Clear! Dry! A single large clearing on the northwest side. Have a care for the huge red oaks! Furbetrance suggests we try it."

"Go for it!" Tom shouted back. "Hang on, ladies! Might be a bit rough, Blackly!"

Furbie braked, whipping his long tail about to steer. He slowed to—perhaps, Tom thought—twenty miles an hour.

Which is slow for a forty-five foot Dragon.

"Not so fast..." Retruance began to warn his younger brother.

"That's not...!" Hetabelle screamed.

"Stop! Bail up! Abort..." Tom bellowed in his loudest non-librarian roar.

"...water, at all!" Hetabelle finished, but a terrific dash and crash—and a *whooomp!* drowned her words as Furbie hit the green surface.

"*Oh!*" cried Manda. "Furbetrance! Are you hurt?"

The great blue Dragon shook his head free of about five thousand water lily pads, blew a startled blast of orange flame, then rolled over on his back and waved all four feet in the air.

At which moment there were two smaller explosions of wet greenery and tea-tinted water as Bravura and Gonerell plunged with gleeful screams into the lily pond.

"He's fine, Mama! Warm as bath water—and we all need baths, I imagine!" Bravura called.

"I'm just...sort of surprised. Who ever saw water lilies so thick?"

"But we would prefer dry—or at least a bit less wet—campsite, Furbetrance!" Manda called. "See what's available now you're down there, anyway."

There was no clear area on the whole hummock. Retruance and his brother combined yellow and blue flames in great sharp jets to clear and then bake dry a half-acre at the highest point of land.

To cool the site, Hetabelle and her daughters scooped up sand and scrubbed the new campsite until it was clean.

Tom checked. "Dry and firm! Baked the sand almost to concrete."

"Everybody into the water or onto the open field," Retruance called out. "Tents in case it gets cold again—although it's pretty warm, right now."

"Supper in an hour," Manda announced. "Yes, Gay, if your father says so, you may swim, too. Stay near the Dragons! Who knows what nasty, hungry beasties live in these waters."

"The water's clean and shallow. Sand bottom," Blackly told Gay. "Wait until they pile up these pads washed ashore by Furbie's crash landing."

It did snow, beginning about dessert time, but before then Hummock Camp was cozy and tight and proof against the new snowfall.

The temperature drooped until Gay and the dog could amuse themselves by blowing *Dragon's Breath* rings before Manda called them into the warm tent for bed.

"This would be great fun…if Brenda were here," the little Princess said sadly. "Where do you think she can be, Papa?"

"Not far away. We'll search for her more after breakfasting tomorrow, my pet. A seagoing ship with two tall masts and all those sails should be easy to spot, even in this weather."

"I'm not as hopeful as you," Manda murmured after he'd slipped into their sleeping bag beside her. "And the invaders, whoever they may be? I haven't forgotten them."

"I think they may be connected. The invaders paid some pirates to kidnap a princess to hold against Carolna's surrender. They caught the miller's daughter instead."

"Good a theory as any." His wife sighed. "But that makes it even *more* dangerous, doesn't it? I mean—our enemy may be as confused and lost as are we!"

"The worst thing you can do is lay awake and worry about it," Tom soothed her. "Go to sleep! We'll talk it over again tomorrow."

But he lay awake for a long while, mulling the whole matter over and over again in his mind.

When the sun rose, the six Constable Dragons and Flo stirred and shook off any ice that had stuck on their wings with much sizzling, thumping, and some girlish giggles.

Little Charlie wandered down to the shore for a drink, bubbled playfully for a moment, then lifted her pink head high into the air.

"Mama? Papa? Someone's coming!"

Blackly and Retruance ran down to the pond, sniffing the swamp air carefully.

"I catch it! What do you think, shepherd? You've got the best nose of the lot, here."

"I smell—another Dragon! He was with us a few days ago, I believe. Young—what was his name?—Brazier!"

Hetabelle joined them. "My sonny Brazier! From the south, he comes! Wake Tom and Manda, brother-in-law. I catch the scent of the Woodsman Clem and one other, also."

Tom emerged from the tent, pulling on his fleece jacket.

"Brazier and Clem? That'll likely be Byron Boldface with them."

"Yes, I remember the scent of the Tiki," Retruance and Flo said as one. "Too far off to see us or smell us against the wind, so far, Tom."

"Stoke up the fire and dump on some of the damp lily pads—for smoke. They'll see that before they can sight us, I think."

Brazier, mistaking the lily pond for a lawn just as his father had, splashed-in and came ashore snorting and blowing like a whale.

"Well met!" Furbetrance hailed. "A lesson to learn, my son. Always circle a landing place at least once before touching down."

"Ah, well, Papa—a cold shower and a warm welcome combined. Hello all! Greetings Mama and Sisters. Princesses and Sir Tom! Uncle Retruance? Was it Papa that made this hole in the lily-pads, or you?"

"Never mind, youngster." Retruance couldn't hide a puff of delighted laughter. "Tiki Boldface and Clem Herronsson come up for some hot breakfast and we'll say no more about splash-down landings."

"Eat, drink strong coffee and tell us everything you've done, Tiki, since you left your warm shore." Tom also laughed aloud.

"We thought to find an enemy here, and found friends, rather," Byron said when Tom helped him to a seat by the fire. "Breakfast! It's always tastier when someone else cooks it. *Three* teaspoons of sugar, if you please,

Princess Manda!"

While the new arrivals ate and sipped steaming coffee, Tom and then Clem described in details their adventures since leaving Carolna.

"And you've decided to track down the kidnappers, first," Clem said, nodding. "I agree. Rescue the little maid. I've been thinking for some days the weather we've been having lately must slow down any invasion force, as well as us."

"Except Dragons," Gay insisted. "Brenda need not fear. My Papa and our Dragons and you will un-nap her and punish those wicked nippers!"

A thousand or so miles to the east—and a length south—of Lexor, an exhausted Crossbeak fluttered through an open window of Palmshade Auditorium on the sunny southeast coast of Carolna, flopped wearily across the dusty stage to the podium, and collapsed on Arcolas' smudged and dog-eared script.

"Message for me?" Murdan's wizard-physician gasped in surprise.

The Crossbeak muttered irritably but nodded his gray head.

"Excuse me, honored colleagues I have received..."

Arcolas glanced at the note he'd un-strapped from the bird's right leg. He then read it again more slowly, frowning.

"Go on without me, fellows! We from Carolna are recalled!"

He scooped up his papers, his reading glasses, a handful of chalk sticks in various colors, and stuck them all in his pockets.

As an afterthought he lifted the sleeping bird and placed it—her—in his skull-cap.

And walked off stage without a backward glance.

The scholarly assembly gaped and coughed and then broke into noisy conversation, mostly objections.

At stage right a placard reading...

WEATHER

Servant or Master?

--0--

Questions, Observations

& Conclusions

by Illustrious Mage

ARCOLAS OF OVERHALL

...was swept to the floor by a playful gust of hot southern air.

CHAPTER SIXTEEN
The Mighty Diamond

"Follow the river—or split up?" Clem wanted to know. "Tiki, here, says when Hintooans get hit by bad luck, they tend to blame everybody else and everybody else's gods for it."

Tom handed him an ancient, much-wrinkled chart.

"Not much to choose from. Deep-sea sailors evidently never go very far up any of these rivers. And the Diamond is the largest river…they *think*."

"Stay together. Spread wide only when necessary. But are we looking for Brenda? Or the invaders?"

"Brenda, for many reasons, poor child!" Manda put in. "Besides, gentlemen, Brenda we know is a real, live—one hopes—person in danger. The invaders are a rumor only, so far."

"You hit my feeling on that perfectly, sweetheart," Tom agreed. "Find Brenda!"

"I vote for Brenda!" piped Gay, who had been listening to the discussion very carefully.

"You have a valid vote, little Princess." Her father laughed. "Dishes done and tents stowed? We're ready to fly."

"You look a little ashen, I think," Tom said to Manda once they were aloft. "Are you unwell?"

"No, not really. Well…I felt queasy again when I first arose…but a good breakfast soothed it away."

Tom helped her to Retruance's broad head and made sure she and Gay were safely seated and warmly wrapped.

"I feel—a sort of *unease*," the great Dragon said when Tom was seated. "Can you account for it, Companion?"

"I suspect I do," Tom replied and he turned to look back at his wife beside the Dragon's after-right-hand ear. "Do you have something to say about that, Princess Alix Amanda Trusslo-Whitehead? What's amiss?"

Manda first shook her head but then turned the gesture into a reluctant nod.

"I—I—*think* I'm with child. Cramps in the legs? Sick before breakfast? A little dizzy, betimes. I've been such as this before. I'm so sorry, Tom!"

"No need to be anything but absolutely delighted, even here and now, Manda! Is there anything you desire? Anything you crave?"

Manda laughed aloud and threw him a kiss.

"If I *am* pregnant, love-sick Librarian, it hasn't gotten *that* far."

"It isn't too late to send you home. Hetabelle would be more than willing, I'm sure, to carry you and Gay back to Hidden Canyon."

"No! Let us save Brenda, first of all. Then we'll talk of this again. Go!"

Retruance, Gay, and Blackly listened wide-eyed to this exchange but made no comment. The Dragon signaled to Furbetrance to fly closer.

"Tell all to pick the smoother airs and softer winds, as much as possible. Manda thinks she is with child! Don't shake her up if we can avoid it."

Furbie, an old hand with a pregnant wife after five children, nodded silently but blew a thin, white wisp of smoke before he charged off upwind to tell the news.

The hunt resumed, following the frozen Diamond toward the west-northwest, across the wide, white coastal plain toward low black hills beyond. The day had turned clear and not nearly as cold.

"Mama? Is the new baby inside you a *brother* or a *sister?*" Gay asked.

"No telling. You'll be the first to know—after your father, my dearest."

"And—what can I do to help, Mama?"

"Be your own true, helpful, good-natured, sweet, smart, pretty, polite, curious daughter—just as you always are. There may come a time when I'll need a woman's comfort and assistance. When that happens—*if* that happens—I'll call on you, first of all."

"Yes, Mama."

"For now? Keep a sharp eye on the Diamond River, below. We need to find that sloop and rescue our friend."

"Oh, yes, Mama!" said the child with sure enthusiasm. "I'll watch very carefully!"

CHAPTER SEVENTEEN
The Red City

Brenda stood amidships and watched the sailors swabbing the sloop's foredeck, trying not to shiver in the wet, chill wind. She still wore tattered pieces of the gown, coat and leggings she had worn in Wall, assisted by an outsized pair of sailor's trews, rolled up at the ankles.

Her single long black braid had already been shorn short by Crippen's pocketknife on the insistence of Fats the Cook.

"I'm not the ocean's greatest cook," he admitted as Crippen wielded his blade. "But I knows to keep me slumgullions clear o' crab shells and dirty hair. Captain bites a bit o' your braid, we *both* might get tossed to the sharks. And you, too, Crippen!"

The boy shook the heavy folding knife irritably. "Sit still and don't whine!"

"I'm *not* whining!" Brenda retorted. "*Ouch!* You're way too rough!"

"Cut your own, hereafter, missy!" Crippen growled, good-naturedly.

"Must stick a straw in the Captain's devil's-food cake," she said, pulling away. "See if it's baked."

She found a pair of scissors and snipped away more of her filthy locks making them look as boyish as possible—out of self-defense.

A crewman, catching her alone hanging dish rags out to dry, had made a leering suggestion—she was common-born enough to understand very well what he wanted—and she had turned him firmly away with a veiled threat.

"There're some nasty-smelling things came up in the nets today. Be careful Cookie doesn't see you get 'em in your mess, tonight."

Fats was Brenda's protector and Captain Downpour chose not to interfere.

Besides, he had an idea even a Princess would lose ransom value, if despoiled.

"Has this river got a name?" Brenda asked while scrubbing the last few potatoes.

"I hear," Fats chirped cheerfully, " 'tis called...*Diamond River*. Or was it *Sapphire?*"

"Diamond," said the ship's boy. "Largest river in Hintoo, the Captain says."

"When—*if*—I get home," Brenda vowed, "I am going to take up geography. Lord Murdan has at least a score of geography books on one self."

"A *score!* Ain't that many books in all the world!" Crippen snorted.

"Tell me; can you read, Crippen?" Fats chuckled.

"A word here and there," the lad said stoutly. "Me own name, read *and* write!"

"This lass, ye hear me? Reads like a wizard! I learn recipes from her just remembering her mother's printed book."

"Well—she's a gentle-woman! What do you expect? Her kind runs the whole world."

"Dad's a blacksmith," Brenda snorted. "He's not gentry."

"Depends on your point of looking, up or down, I 'spect," Fats said. "Run and fetch..."

A lookout far above hailed, "Deck! *Deck!* Thar's Jewelbox! Jewelbox 'round the point, Captain Downpour, sir!"

"First port-o'-call since Wall," Fats muttered. "Let's hope we gets some vittles, here. I'm sick to tired from smelling fish a-frying!"

"So are we all," Crippen shouted. "C'mon, Brenda! Let's take a look at 'er."

It was a small city built mostly of red bricks set in uneven courses and wavy patterns. In the center, crowning a low hill, rose a square-towered keep of deep crimson stone. Its walls reflected a ruddy glow and they had obviously once been highly polished.

"No flags flying!" Brenda said.

"And no one abroad, anywhere!" said Crippen.

Winter-naked red maples and yellow willows lined the river bank, and winter-brown weeds, thistles and dry grasses grew everywhere, even between the pink paving stones of the riverfront wharfs, on the dark slate roofs of cavernous warehouses, and the shops and houses along narrow, winding streets.

"Been here before," Cookie told them quietly. "Still—impressive, I'd call it. Man told me it was once a precious metals and gemstones market for all Hintoo. Been empty for a century or so," he said.

"Why's it empty, though?" Brenda whispered. Something about the city of red brick and deep red stone made her speak in a low tone. "It's rather—*pretty*."

"I heard stories…" Cook said. "Later on, perhaps I'll tell you. The Bloody History of Swang Kwo."

"Swang Kwo?"

"*Blood Stone*—*ah,* a ruby, you might say. Or so I've been told."

The three friends stood inside the galley hatch where they wouldn't be noticed and watched Downpour, armed with everything from a short sword to six long dirks tucked in his belt, emerge from his cabin, aft.

"Lower the longboat!"

"I still don't see a sign of Cobra…or 'is crew," muttered his First Mate. He studied the wharves with a spyglass. "Gave 'im plenty o' warning!"

Downpour shook his head and snatched the glass from his mate.

"You got to learn *patience*, Noose! You stay here, in command. Listen, you swabbies! Gal's worth a hat-full o' coin to each man here. Don't bollix things up! You, Hoity! Drop best bower! Better if we don't tie *Updraft* to a dock."

"Aye, aye, Capt'n!" yelled petty officer Hoity.

He in turn screamed an order and Brenda, for the first time, heard the anchor chain rattle through the starboard hawse and boom into the water.

"Let's show ourselves, then," the Captain decided. Six armed oarsmen and his coxswain dropped into the longboat. Then he clambered over the side and ordered the line cast off.

"Give 'way! Lay into it, you lubbers! Steer for them stairs, cox'n!"

Five strokes of the sweeps took the boat ashore at a flight of stone steps climbing the mall. Downpour and his men climbed from the boat while the cox'n busied himself mooring her to a stone bollard.

The crew on board lined the rail, watching and muttering…Brenda decided…a bit fearfully.

They watched a black-clad group—ten figures armed with short, re-curved bows—suddenly appear from behind one of the warehouses and confront the shore party.

"Who *are* they?" Brenda whispered.

"Don't know what they're called, but I'd guess…bandits," Fats said. "Whoever they are, they're the ones paid for your snatching."

All watched the two armed parties in silence, now, trying to decipher what was being said from gestures and head movements.

The black officer, evidently the one called Cobra, shook a fist at Downpour—in anger, they thought.

"He wants to know where *I* am!" Brenda said with a shudder, feeling a stab of cold fear shoot down her back.

Downpour shook his head sharply and waved both arms above his head. His shore party crowded behind him, fingering cutlasses and belaying pins nervously.

Or so it seemed.

The black-clad archers notched long arrows and prepared to draw their bows.

CHAPTER EIGHTEEN
Meanwhile, Back at Overhall

Completely at a loss to do more to prepare Carolna for war with an unknown invader, the King and his Historian sat before a sea coal fire in Alix Amanda Alone Palace.

"Enough to drive one stark crazy!" Murdan groaned. "What to *do?* What *else* to do!"

"Wait!" Eduard shrugged wearily. "Just wait! Hurry—and then wait."

"I can't just sit here waiting. I'd make a very bad King, I suppose. I should stay here by your side and wait on events. Spring will come, eventually.

"But I really feel I should go home and do some reading. What Tom calls research? Somewhere could I find such things happening before?"

Eduard wasn't listening.

"Beatrix and Ednol are at Knollwater until comes spring, now. They'll be safe there—and warmer."

"Overhall will be a lump of ice. But if I can..."

There came a discrete knock on the chamber door. At the King's call of "Enter!" Lord Chamberlain Walden slipped through and bowed to him.

"Your Majesty! My Lord Historian's Wizard-Physician Arcolas has arrived. He says you sent for him, Lord Murdan."

"Of *course* I did, dammit! Bring him in—*er*—if it's your will, Eduard."

"Send him in!" Eduard snorted. "You've been looking for him for more than a fortnight!"

Arcolas, a bedraggled figure still wet from melted snow on his narrow shoulders, bowed respectfully to the monarch and then to his employer, the Historian of Overhall.

"Where in the ever-loving, fire-blasted, dog-eared hell have *you* been?" Murdan shouted. "What have you to say before I fire you out of hand? Or post you to Frontier to tend sick horses? Or have you hung for desertion!"

Arcolas bowed again. He didn't look too worried about the possibilities the Historian suggested.

"I was Lead Guest and Primary Speaker at the annual wintertime *Seminar for Mages, Witches and Wizards* in Palmshade—as I *told* you, Lord Historian, in person and in a detailed memo dated the twentieth of November…"

"Seminar!" Murdan began to swear but then he laughed and grinned ruefully. "In all the excitement, I *completely* forgot! Forgive me, Arcolas!"

"Not anything to forgive, m'lord," the medical Mage murmured. "You sent for me and I have come—at great trouble, some danger, and much discomfort, I might add."

"Of course you did, old boy, and we really appreciate it," Eduard said. "Carolna needs all the help we can get, Doctor!"

"The weather or the invaders, is it? Both certainly troublesome, sir! I heard of them first at Knollwater, where I stopped two nights ago. Her Highness and children send their love and concern, incidentally."

"Thank you, Doctor. You found them well?"

"Except for missing your company, Majesty, they are perfectly well."

"Your master and I hope you can assist us in these matters of our concern."

"Concern? We're frightened out of our skins, nearly!" Murdan said, more calmly now. "Your arrival, old friend, is most welcome. Get yourself warmed up and wrung out and get some hot supper."

"Ah, yes, I will, m'lord!"

"A sound night's sleep, also, would be a good idea. If you can sleep, after I tell you all what's going on."

"Thank you, sir!"

"And be ready to fly by Dragon to Overhall with me at first light tomorrow!"

After the wet Wizard sloshed off, King Eduard Ten laid his hand fondly on his half-brother's shoulder.

"A boon, Murdan?"

"Of course, Eduard. *For King and Country,* as they say. "

"Take me along, please! Perhaps…"

"…perhaps you can help? You could've demanded it, but since you asked nicely I say, again, 'Of course!' "

He hugged his brother and turned to shout to a messenger outside the closed door.

"Find my Dragon! Tell him we—King, Mage and me—leave for Overhall in the morning. He'll carry us."

"How about a nice supper for us, too, after we've packed?" the King suggested. "In this kind of weather—raining now, I see—I'd like buckwheat pancakes drowned in maple syrup, lots of sweet butter and little pig sausages. And a pot of steaming coffee!"

In an age and a world where it took people three weeks to travel from Lexor to Overhall Castle, a Dragon was a convenience of the first order. Altruance fought strong northwest headwinds and still made the trip in two days and a night.

The King, the Historian, and the Wizard fared fairly comfortably under thick northern bearskins and double-knit woolen underwear. Murdan ordered stops of a few hours at Lakehead for a hot meal and overnight at Ffallmar Farm to visit his daughter Rosemary and his grandchildren.

"Will you come with us to Overhall?" Murdan asked his daughter. "You'd be much safer, dear heart. And I won't feel as uncertain."

"No, Papa, my duty and my heart lie here at Ffallmar Farm. Perhaps, when the war starts, I can bring everybody within your high walls. I'll talk with my soldier-husband, first."

Murdan sighed. "I was thinking of myself, of course. I do feel lonely at times like these."

"But you have Uncle Eduard! And you have important work to do. No, I'll stay with my people."

"So be it, then! Oh, consider sending us a wagon—or a sleigh—train with food. I suspect we may get very hungry, before spring. If spring ever comes!

"Spring will come, I believe. With my handsome Ffallmar in command? We *will* prevail."

Her father wiped away a small tear and embraced her in farewell. Eduard also hugged her, and her children, Eddie, Valery, and Molly, crowded close to say goodbye to their Grand Uncle Eduard as well as Grampa Murdan.

They were a bit more shy saying fare-ye-well to Arcolas. Their mother threw her arms about the Magi and said, "We depend on you, dear Doctor! Keep them well and whole, please."

"I'd give my life for them, I promise you, if it would keep them well."

"Altruance, I know I can depend on you to guard."

She carefully kissed the older Constable Dragon on his hot nose, deftly avoiding a puff of embarrassed pink steam. He patted her on the shoulder with a huge and sharp red talon.

"I have such great memories of you, when you were new-hatched," he sniffed. "You remember how to call me, if danger comes to Ffallmar Farm?"

"I remember that, be sure." Rosemary laughed. "Now, Papa! You can't make it home before full dark if you delay further."

"We're going," Murdan agreed, giving her one last kiss and again patting his grandchildren on their heads. "I'll see you again, come spring!"

In a blaze of gold and green sunset—the first sunset seen in weeks of storm clouds—Arbitrance wheeled above Overhall, dipped his great wings in salute, and glided to a weary but careful landing in Middle Bailey.

Glad cheers, cries of relief and welcome-home by a crowd of Overhall officials, servants, shepherds, kitchen maids, stable boys, craftsmen and soldiers greeted the tired travelers.

Murdan greeted his housekeeper Mistress Grumble and saluted Grey Grahamsson, now a full Lieutenant of the Overhall Guard.

"Supper, a good night's sleep, and I have work to begin in the morning, dear people! It's *very* good to be safe within these old walls, once again."

CHAPTER NINETEEN
Historian Studies History

Waking two hours late the next morning, Murdan swore happily at his valet Flaretty.

"*No!* Not the fancy stuff, boy! Anything will do. I have work to do."

"Your bath, Lord Murdan?"

"No time! *No time!*"

"Please, sir! You *must*. You stink."

The Historian started to snarl a rejoinder, but gulped down his anger.

"You're right, of course, Flaretty. A fast dip, then. Have it drawn. Hot! But send for Graham, first of all."

The valet turned away, assuring him a tub of hot water and soap awaited...and then turned back.

"Commander Graham is gone. He answered the Call to Arms from Lord Ffallmar. He left his son Greysolon as his lieutenant, sir."

"Get the damn lad! Graham gone? Ah, well...shampoo-to-toenails in ten minutes! That's an *order*, sirrah!"

He shed nightshirt, nightcap, and slippers as he dashed into his bathing room.

"*Is it cool enough!*" someone warned him.

"Cool be blasted! Scrub!"

Young Grey came in a few minutes later, breathless from a hurried climb to Murdan's suite in full armor.

"Reporting, Lord Historian!"

"Take off your cloak and some steelwork and sit down for a moment, laddy. Your father left the castle-guarding duties to you?"

"Yes, he did, sir. He took the Sergeant with him."

"I believe you're the best-suited, since he has so decided. Relax! Tell, what is the condition of our defenses? How many Guardsmen went east to Ffallmar's muster? Wherever *that* is."

Grey allowed the valet's boy to strip off his wet cloak—and his jacket, shirt and trousers, stockings and small-clothes, too. He was soaked to the skin.

"Commander took three of the five companies, Lord Historian. Twenty men—archers mostly—in each. Total of sixty. On foot, except for Papa—*uh*, the Commander—and his Sergeant Major."

"Well, this place was Dragon-built to be held by just a few good men. And the reserves?"

"All armed and drilled daily since muster-call came. They'll do well. Many of the older men have served before and remember how it works!"

"With good leadership. Not like the time I foolishly took *all* my soldiers and went off to Lexor."

"As for the battlements, walls and gates? Overhall's as tight as *any* fortress ever was. We're chock full of food. Plenty of firewood, yet. And hay and straw. Gugglerun never entirely freezes, as you know. Gods know we'll not be short of water."

Murdan climbed out of the tub, dripping soapy water on the tiles. An assistant valet began to dry him vigorously with a huge towel.

"I leave it to you, then. Report anything untoward or unexpected that happens," said the naked Historian. "I suppose I should inspect them, at least."

"You can do it at Evening Parade, if you wish. Yes, I think it a good idea. Men'll appreciate it."

Dried and dressed—he even agreed to be shaved—Murdan ordered breakfast brought to him in his study. He drank two cups of powerful black coffee and ate a number of toast points with strawberry jam at his desk.

"Get along then, and don't let anybody bother me," he ordered his staff, "unless there's word I should hear or things I should know at once."

They bobbed heads quickly and trooped out, taking the breakfast dishes—but not the pot of coffee—with them.

"*Now!*"Murdan coughed. "What is it I should do? Start with the *Carolna Almanacs*, I suppose. I do wish I had my Librarian handy."

He lifted three heavy volumes to his reading table and ran a handkerchief over them before he could handle the dusty books further.

"Get Arcolas, you there!" he shouted at the closed door. "I need some professional help here."

The Wizard-Doctor must have been waiting outside, for he appeared at once.

"I need an estimate of the depth of snowfall since late December," said the Historian, already smudged with book dust, "Do it at once!"

"Yes, Librarian! How...?"

"*Your* problem, Arcolas. I want to compare snowfalls of past years. Since records began, if I can."

Arcolas nodded and went to another part of the study to do his fact-seeking, so as not to disturb the Historian.

"Here at Overhall, an annual average of fifty-three inches of new-fallen snow. Average night temperatures ran around freezing. Total may be slightly lower. It got above freezing point several days recently. Figure an inch of snow to ten inches of rain—but nobody ever bothered to measure rainfall in January," the Wizard reported.

"Hereafter I want all rain *and* snow measured, all year. See if you can find someone to do it properly."

"Findles of Aquanelle, Historian?"

"*Good!* His interest is water—lakes, rivers, tides, springs, swamps, wells, rainfall. Make a note to write him as soon as you can get mail through this blasted snow.

"Now figure Lexor and Wall or some place on the west coast. Herron, Clem's father, may have some idea. He owns a small coastal fleet; he should know his weather pretty well."

"Take a few minutes," was the Wizard's reply.

"Do it! I'll start to compare past records nearer to home."

Ten hours later the Lord of Overhall found his Dragon talking with off-duty castle people around a roaring bonfire in Fore Bailey.

"I must take you away from your fireside chatting," he said to Arbitrance. "I need a longish message sent to Retruance for Tom, wherever they may be."

"Will and can do it, at once, Companion! Folks? I give up the pleasure of firelight and warm hands and faces while I heed the call of duty. Excuse me!"

"I'll keep it short. Tom will understand. You ready?"

"Dictate away. I'll transmit, Companion."

"To Retruance for Tom Librarian: "Six times in the past century Carolna has had cold as low and long, and snowfall as great, if not greater, than this current winter. All six appear purely natural, not due to anybody's magic.""

Arbitrance nodded and whistled a thin jet of surprised white steam. "Not magical! But..."

"Just send those words, old lizard. Tom's my expert in non-magical phenomena. We'll wait to hear from him. Bright lad, that Whitehead."

He turned away to head for the castle kitchen for some late supper.

"Breakfast, actually," he said to himself. "I missed Evening Parade, after I promised! And supper!"

CHAPTER TWENTY
The Ice Dragon Cometh

Gay lay on her tummy with her chin resting on folded arms, watching the ice-spattered river slide steadily below. "I'm surprised the great river is not over-frozen."

"Water's moving too fast," Blackly explained.

He was lying close beside her, sharing the warmth and the view from Retruance's broad head.

"Like Gugglerun." The little princess nodded.

She'd grown up beside rivers—Gugglerun at Overhall Castle, the long, lazy Cristol River which ran from near Lakehead across the plains to Mantura Bay on the Peaceful Ocean; and—her very favorite—the bright, clear, stone-bottomed Julia Creek that ran past Hidden Canyon House and disappeared in the desert to the east. It was named for a certain fiercely proud, powerful lady jaguar with a heart of pure gold.

"Papa?" Gay called over her shoulder. "Oh, Papa! Furbetrance is waving! He's seen something."

Tom swung his spyglass about to find Furbie, far out front.

"Spotted a city on the river!" a young Constable female called out.

"It must be the one on your old map, Tiki," Retruance said. "What was it called? Something about—rubies?"

Byron called from Flo's head. "It means 'Blood Stone City.' I have never been there but I have heard curious tales of it. Very wealthy. Very powerful! A marketplace for all kinds of precious stones, but ages ago."

Furbetrance swooped up, over, and back. "It looks—well—*deserted!*

Sort of. No chimney smoke—in this cold weather? No small craft at the docks?"

"What color is the city," Byron called.

"Yellow, mostly. *No!* Red and yellow. Mostly red, with all those bricks," Furbie said.

"That will be Swang Kwo. No other city on the Diamond has red brick walls."

"We'll look it over—later. But carefully," Tom decided. "All these Dragons flying in a line? We couldn't sneak up on a blind cave fish!"

"A bit of leg-stretching and dinner are in order, first," Manda insisted. "There's a clear, dry patch down to the right. Green grass! When did we see green grass last?"

The line of Dragons curved gracefully down to the grassy hilltop. First passenger to dismount was Blackly, who ran about in excited circles, sniffing eagerly, stopping frequently to look about intently.

"Seems quite clear," he barked to the others. "Some little critters have been about since the snow stopped…and sheep have grazed here, recently. I can smell 'em! Come on down, all."

"If there are sheep," Manda said as she stepped from Retruance's left forepaw, "there are bound to be shepherds. Jump carefully, Gay! Oh, I wish I were as young and nimble as you."

"Shepherds are usually peaceful and honest people, I've found," Blackly said to Clem.

"I'll take a walk-about," the Woodsman promised. "Soon as Furbie starts the fire. Plenty of kindling on down the slope, I see."

"I'll tag along. If you allow it—just to be sure it's safe," Furbetrance told him. "But the old nose doesn't catch any suspicious stinks, hereabouts."

"We'll go, too," Tom told Gay. "As mama says, get the kinks out of our legs a bit."

The other Dragons settled down, amazingly merging colors with the green of the new grass, the brown and yellow of fallen leaves, and the grey of winter-bare trees about the meadow.

"Will need some water!" Manda called after them. "We'll have to be satisfied with soup, today, and crackers. Meat is scarce!"

But they were already too far off to hear.

"Menfolk!" exclaimed Hetabelle, more in fondness than irritation.

"Always running off, looking for trouble, leaving us womenfolk with the cooking to do.

"Here, girls! I smell fresh water down there to the left. Bring enough for soup and drinking—and some bathing, too."

Brass Nose led her sisters down to a hidden spring at the foot of the rise carrying collapsible canvas buckets, each big enough to be a man's bathtub.

They filled them each carefully, to avoid scooping up dead leaves and floating sticks. On her way back to the campsite, Brass Nose warmed her bucket with her hot breath, while the others lifted their buckets to their heads to keep them chilled.

Manda first tasted the water, pronounced it quite clear and good-tasting, then filled the big soup pot from Bravura's bucket which began to boil almost at once.

"All the conveniences of home—except for a professional chef," she sang happily. "Lunch in a half an hour at most, children."

When the soup was gone and the last of the crackers eaten, Tom and Retruance again climbed to the top of the hill to look around. Brass Nose, Gorgonzola, Baby Sister and Chartreuse gathered tiny, heavenly-blue violets blooming in the new grass.

Young Brazier lay on his back in the soft grass—half asleep if truth be told—practicing blowing purple smoke-rings into the still, cool air.

He suddenly sat bolt upright, snorted a jet of warning black and cried out, "Papa! Tom! *Everybody!* A Dragon is coming. An *awful big, steaming pale blue beastie…*"

Tom swiveled to where Brazier pointed. Retruance snorted grey steam, himself, and growled.

"I think I've met this one before!" Tom exclaimed, shading his spyglass from the midday sun. "Isn't that the Ice Dragon once saved Murdan and Peter Gantrell from freezing to death?"

"So it is!" both Retruance and Clem cried out in relief.

"*Hoarling Frostbite!* Come on down, Hoarling! We're holding a Dragon's Conventicle, here in Hintoo!" Tom added.

"Barely bearable, this damn warm weather of yours," complained the Ice Dragon, thumping irritably to a landing. The cold, white breath of his nearness withered the young grass at once. "I suppose it'll get worse, now

I'm here, Librarian. It seems to always gets hot when I fly south."

"You should have been here a week ago, frost lizard," Retruance chuckled. "Welcome, anyway! We greatly need your help and sweet tempers."

"I came as soon as I heard your call," said the Ice Dragon, ignoring Retruance's greeting. "What's the matter? What are you and Princess Manda—and all these Constable creatures—doing here, so far from home?"

"Right now we're chasing a band of sea marauders who've snatched a child of my household. We've traced the sour scum this far—to the red city upstream."

"I recall visiting Blood Stone—or whatever they call it—but then it was a pretty wild town, filled with loud noises and violence, gambling and mayhem and such delightful carry-ons!"

"They seem to have run off, for some reason," Tom said. "We're about to scout about a bit. See if we can tell where everybody went—and why."

"I'll join your party—since you asked nicely. I'd like to know, also. The Hintoos who lived here were as close to my kind of scoundrel as any."

"Feed your curiosity," Retruance snorted. "There are two problems to be solved and I think you can be of some help. Drive off the mosquitoes, for example?"

"Nasty Constable! Biting bugs are good, old friends of us cold critters. Many a late summer's night I've fallen asleep to the tune of their hungry whining!"

"If we guessed right," Manda quickly interrupted, "the town is called Swang Kwo. Agreed?"

"Agree, Princess! Full of rascally jewelers, cheating stone-cutters and thieving goldsmiths. They gave the name to River Diamond, but their real passion is—*was*—rubies! Lovely, cold, hard, clear red stones! I'm prepared to fly when you people are ready."

"We won't see anything until morning light," Manda insisted. "Supper and sleep, first! We can't offer you ice cream, Hoarling, but perhaps some iced tea?"

"I haven't had a sip of that inspiring invention of your countrymen in years, Princess! And ol' Blood Stone ain't going nowhere."

While they sat around the fire eating cheese and crackers with their soup and drinking strong tea—choice of hot or iced—twilight faded into full night.

The Ice Dragon turned to Tom. "I suggest a night reconnaissance, eh? Spot fires and lights better at night."

"Good idea! Take Retruance and young Brazier with you. Be back before midnight. I'll wait up for you. My Companion and his nephew will fill you in on our double mission."

Long experience with Dragons had taught him to assign the great, winged, wakeful beasts something useful to do while others slept—and to give them clear, careful instructions about doing it.

"Observe only! Don't touch unless you must! Remember, somewhere ahead of us is a terrified little girl being held captive."

"Understood, Companion dear," Retruance said, spreading his wings. "You go first and a bit above, Frostbite. That way you'll avoid the warmth of our slipstreams."

"How very thoughtful!" Hoarling huffed. "I can be the largest target if someone starts to shoot."

Gay, who had been studying the stranger Dragon she had never met before, clapped her hands.

"Brave Hoarling! Save my Brenda and bring her safe to Overhall in the end!"

"Who was *that?*" Hoarling asked Retruance as they rose into the night's darkness. "*Another* maid-in-waiting?"

Retruance waited until they had gained altitude over the Diamond before he replied.

"She's Tom's and Manda's daughter. You last came to Overhall, she was not yet a tiny nestling, I suppose. Her name is Gale because she was born at sea during a hurricane."

"Oh?"

"Everybody calls her Gay, because at ten years, she's ever a bright bit of sunshine even on coldest, darkest, most stormy days."

"Nobody explained her to me. I'm sorry, Retruance. I truly am!"

They flew several miles before the Ice Dragon spoke again.

"If I understand you a-right," he said thoughtfully, "she is a Princess?"

Brazier, trailing dutifully behind his uncle, laughed. "Princess Royal Gale Amanda Whitehead of Carolna and Hidden Canyon. I think she likes you, Hoarling! It was you she cheered as we took off."

Hoarling Frostbite pretended to ignore the lad's comment and said little more until the scouting flight circled over the deserted, cold, silent, dark streets of the jeweler's city on the Diamond.

"*Ah-ha!*" Retruance said suddenly. "There by he riverside, y' see." That must be the kidnapper's ship. It's a Carolnan craft, for sure."

"Yes, I've seen her likes before. A sloop, I think. Or is it called schooner?"

"I see her now for the first time. We've been following her at sea blind for most of a week! Can you read her name painted on her rump, there?"

Hoarling slid down almost to the wharf, making no noise at all despite his speed, then banked steeply to the left and climbed to where Retruance and Brazier circled above.

"Says *Updraft* on 'er sternboard," he reported. "And from the looks of 'er, she's deserted. No light. No smoke."

"I'll take a closer look," decided Retruance. "Stay aloft and give us a hiss if you see anyone coming, Brazier! Keep eyes and ears open wide."

The Dragons skimmed to mast-top level, studying the kidnapper's sagging rigging and empty decks.

When he returned on high, Retruance shook his great, green head. "No light nor fire; not even a lantern, as you say, friend Hoarling. But I'm positive *someone* is there, well below deck."

"Maybe that's where the poor lassie is held," Brazier said. "We must go and rescue her!"

"No, *your* job is fetch Tom and Clem. Perhaps the Tiki, too. 'Tween decks is way too narrow for any of us big people. These are desperate men. They could kill the little girl before we got to them! Tom will know what to do. *Go!*"

The younger Dragon nodded quickly and shot off down the river.

"Do...do you think...?" Hoarling whispered.

"They're either asleep—or *dead*. You see the stone wall off to the right a bit? We'll settle there 'til the menfolk come. Do what we're told. Watch and listen carefully!"

CHAPTER TWENTY-ONE
Doom of Updraft

Tom, Clem, Blackly, and Byron arrived within a half hour. The young men were fully armed and half-armored. Byron carried a heavy knife. The sheep dog growled deep in his throat, his back fur standing stiffly upright.

Tom carried his only sword, the Knight's Sword given him by the King some years before when he had dubbed Tom a Knight of Carolna.

The Woodsman wore a razor-sharp hewing axe in his belt and carried a long bow in his left hand and a quiver of grey goose feathered arrows on his back.

Byron gingerly carried a long, two-handed, curved knife. Tom had seen him split a coconut, husk and all, with a single blow—no mean feat.

"*Hey!* Over here!" came a soft hiss from Retruance, waving the barbed tip of his tail above the wall.

The three men, the dog, and Brazier climbed over the stone wall and sat down in a darkness lighted only by the faint, green glow of Dragons' eyes.

"Nothing to report," Furbetrance told them. "Not a stir nor even a rattle, anywhere. Both here and in the city, also."

"But you're *sure* you felt someone aboard her—below decks? *Updraft*, is she? You ever hear of an *Updraft*, Clem?"

"Never! But then—I don't pay much attention to boat's names."

"She's a *ship*," the Librarian told him. "And a ship's always a *she*. Even when somebody names them *Updraft*."

"We agree *she's* an *eastern* kind of vessel," said the Tiki, "and the type for which we've been searching."

Said Retruance, "She *must* be the kidnapper's ship!"

"And probably her wicked, nasty crew sleeps inside," Hoarling added. "We need only crack 'er in two, I say. Like an egg."

"Hold on, though!" Tom warned them. "If our little girl is aboard…"

"We're stumped, then," his Companion sighed. "If we storm this *Updraft*—if we come down on them full weight like wolves in winter, she could get hurt in the crashing and bashing."

Blackly pressed his cold nose into Tom's hand. "Maybe *I* can tell a bit more, Master Tom. Smell things out?"

"Good idea, but—*carefully!* I seem to be saying that all the time, now. See what you can learn, Blackly. Do you want us come with?"

"*Nay!* Stay here and keep warm by Dragon-snuggling. We'll see what a well-bred Ramhold hound's nose can learn."

And he leapt gracefully over the wall. Fifteen feet into the deep night shadows, Blackly *disappeared!*

The rescue party huddled down, men and Dragons together. A raw breeze stirred, rattling the heavy blocks against the ship's tackle and yards, and whistling softly, mysteriously.

The river rumbled in the background and somewhere in the empty city an owl hooted.

"Can you see him?" Tom wondered.

"Went aboard a moment ago," Retruance whispered. "I don't see him now. I can hear the crewmen snoring. No alarm, yet!"

Even a Dragon's excellent night vision was not sharp enough. The sky was mostly overcast and stars winked on and off fitfully. A quarter moon had set long since.

Almost an hour later the black sheep dog appeared beside them, as silently as he had disappeared.

"Well! Interesting, folks. Good and bad news!"

"Speak!" Retruance snapped, irritated because he'd not detected the dog's quiet return. "Stop your melodrama, dog! Give the facts."

"Give me a chance to catch my breath," Blackly panted. He dropped on his stomach and stuck his pink tongue out at the Dragon.

"Take your time, puppy," Tom said. "Leave him be, Retruance! He'll talk in a moment."

"So it is." Blackly grinned. "First off, the child is not there."

"You're sure?" Furbetrance asked.

"Her smell—*aroma,* if you prefer a politer word—is nowhere near the fo'castle, or whatever it is sailors call their bedrooms. Not now, not been at any time, ever!"

"Elsewhere aboard?" the Librarian asked anxiously.

"Neither whiff nor puff. She's not aboard at all, nor has been in hours. She *has* been there, I smelt—but she is now gone!"

"*Ah,* perhaps—dead?" the Tiki asked in a whisper.

"Not here, at least. She went—or was *taken*—into the city. Through the gate, there, but I haven't followed her trace further, yet. By a gang of strangers—a gang whose smell I don't recognize at all. Horsemen, I *can* say."

Men and Dragons remained silent until Clem stirred, at last, and said, "We can smash the boat—*ship,* I mean. Leave the crew here until after we recover Brenda. They'd *have* to stay stranded. I see no other ships nor even small craft on this riverfront, Tom. And no people, either!"

"The same rule applies," the Librarian agreed. "Brenda comes first and foremost! But…"

He halted the Dragons, all eagerly preparing to take wing and do some serious destruction on *Updraft.*

"We won't actually slay them, I promise," Furbie said. "Just set them ashore…as Clem suggests."

"Knock down their masts?" Clem suggested.

"Better yet," murmured Byron. "Just strip away her sails. She'll go nowhere."

Retruance nodded his great head. "Take us just a moment or two and then we can be off after these new foemen, whoever they are."

Tom said, "Doesn't take four grown Dragons to strip a sloop. Flo, please go and fetch Manda and the rest as soon as day dawns.

"Retruance, you and Hoarling see to the disabling of *Updraft* and disarming her crew. Dismantle, *not destroy*—unless you take kindly to carrying these people home to trial.

"Furbetrance, you, Blackly and I will begin tracking these new kidnappers after we deal with the seamen. But not far beyond 'til everybody is together again. If they're on horseback, they should leave plenty of signs.

"Clem, when the Dragons are finished securing *Updraft,* we'll inform her crew they are under arrest. Or else! Then you'll lead us. We'll want a good, professional tracker.

"Any questions? Then, do it!"

Retruance and his crew rose swiftly into the predawn darkness and circled silent *Updraft* clockwise, lower and lower but quickly.

At first!

Then—the huge beasts began ripping canvas from spars and yards, beginning with the boomed mainsails and then topsails, royals, gallants, jibs and dropping them nearly in a tidy pile on the far bank of the Diamond.

They unraveled all running rigging and added the lines, coiled, to the pile.

Young Brazier watched from quayside to prevent anyone escaping over that side—with hissing blue-white streams of fire waiting to singe toes.

Retruance roared, *"Surrender or die!"*

The fo'castle hatch burst open. Two screaming crewmen attempted to jump to the dock, but Brazier's flames drove them back. Another sailor dove into the swift river current and had to be hooked by sharp Dragon claws and hoisted back to the deck.

Retruance again roared at the top of his considerable voice, "Stand fast! Throw down your weapons! You are under arrest in the name of King Eduard Tenth of Carolna for kidnapping and piracy! Sit down where you are, *immediately*, and don't move a hair or I'll make cinders of you!"

In less than two minutes all was quiet. Clem, followed by Retruance's head and neck, pushed into *Updraft's* dimly-lit fo'castle to face twenty horrified sailors and their captain.

Brazier meanwhile collected swords, cutlasses, pistols, knives, brass knuckles, and belaying pins, and gleefully dropped them into the river—except for the belaying pins, which he neatly replaced in the pin rails at the foot of the masts.

"Now," Tom said quietly when he entered the fo'castle. "I am Sir Thomas Whitehead of Hidden Canyon, Royal Librarian, Librarian of Overhall, husband to Princess Royal Alix Amanda of Carolna, and son-in-law to His Majesty Eduard Tenth Trusslo, King of Carolna."

The captives looked both stunned and even more frightened.

"…and I am the father of Princess Gale of Carolna and Hidden Canyon…"

Gasps of surprise turned into whines of dread. Some seamen dropped to their knees and begged, "Mercy, Lord! *Mercy*, terrible knight! Spare us! We never hurt the child!"

"Makes no difference. The penalties for murder, kidnapping, piracy on the high seas, are all death. I am empowered by my Lord King to hang you all from yardarms immediately!"

"No, *no! Please*, Sir Knight!"

"Which I am fiercely determined to do. Fetch some of that rigging, Hoarling. We'll begin with this wretched captain..."

A tall, thin man stepped forward, ignoring a warning snap of red smoke from Retruance.

"A boon I crave, good Sir Knight! I'm called Fats. Most of us were unaware of any crime until we were well out to sea. Most of us are ordinary seamen. And we did no harm to the little girl—who told me she was not your daughter, at all, but a Lady Brenda, a handmaiden."

"Makes no difference, sirrah! The crime lay in your intention, if not your commission."

"*Not* a Princess!" cried the Captain. "Not a Princess as we thought!"

"You're convicted out of your own mouth," Tom snarled. "Lady Brenda of Sprend is my charge and my responsibility. Her death weighs on me."

"But she is not dead," wailed a youngster, evidently the ship's cabin boy. "She is not here!"

"No, Lord, her capture was for profit to Captain Downpour, as he just confessed. He gave Brenda to those hooded riders! I myself overheard him say they paid well for her capture and delivery."

"I hope she keeps the secret from them!" Tom groaned. "They wanted Gay!"

CHAPTER TWENTY-TWO
Frozen Desert

It was, they found, unnecessary to follow the mysterious black riders on foot. They'd made no effort to hide their tracks.

Blackly had inspected their spoor—as he called their sign—and said there were twenty ridden horses, plus a dozen more without riders.

And they had set off from the red city's north gate at no great speed in a double column. The ground—watery meadows and wet pasturelands now beginning to green—were soft with mud where the deep snow had melted.

"They left Red Stone twenty four hours back," Clem estimated. "At a normal horse's pace, I expect we'll find their first night-camp—*oh,* perhaps twenty miles, or perhaps twenty-five miles ahead. They've headed, as you can see, due north from here."

"We'll fly, then." Tom had decided. "Usual geese-line of flight...and everybody call out any signs. If they see us coming, they may decide to stand and fight—or they may scatter."

"Half-a-mile up and at best Dragon speed?" Retruance recommended. "We'll sight *them* while they'll think us as just a flight of birds in the distance."

"Usual formation," Retruance called to his family and other flying friends. "Keep in line, all. Nobody goes off-line without permission! These baby-snatchers are heavily armed and fully armored, the sailors said. Dangerous to Brenda, if not to us. Let's fly!"

In Lexor the King rode out to review his troops, regulars and reserves, still with no orders for them. His tall and handsome form, riding a magnificent white warhorse, brought his soldiers about to cheer and call his name.

"This is costing Carolna several fortunes," muttered one of the King's advisors.

"We must, however, be prepared, even if nothing happens here," Eduard said firmly. "I'd far rather be beggared by being ready to fight than to be robbed of everything by an unexpected enemy!"

He grinned happily when Ffallmar stood forth to meet them. Louder cheers rose and stayed. Ffallmar saluted the monarch and his royal party and led them to a large tent where a fire burned to warm them.

"Not a word, yet," Eduard said in answer to many questions from his officers. "I've sent my family to Knollwater. I trust your wives and children are safely out of harm's way and well-provisioned?"

"All but my son Eddie, your namesake, Sire. He claimed the right to serve as my page, although he is just fifteen years old."

"It must be a comfort to have him nearby," the King sighed. "My Ednol is still much too young to serve—and he's not happy to be left behind with the ladies!"

Mornie, far to the south, shaded her eyes against the afternoon sun, following a gang of half-naked children playing in a tidal pool nearby.

"A week past," she said to her companions, Parvaiti women of Isthmusi Colony. "I could pick out my lads by their pale backsides—but they already are browning and merging with your youngsters."

"They'll watch your boys as carefully as their own brothers," said one of the mothers with a laugh, bouncing a baby girl on her hip. "Have you heard news today?"

"Only a few words of—well—assurance. My Clem and Tom can take care of themselves. And they have your wonderful Tiki and a whole school—is that right, a *school?*—of Dragons to help."

She chucked the infant under her milk chocolate chin and laughed and then sighed. "I worry, never-the-less."

"Worry is the woman's part, ever," a Parvaiti grandmother told her. "It has ever been that way."

"Good news!" Hoarling barked from high above the line of flight.

"Or—maybe bad news."

"Important to know both kinds." Tom sighed. He stood balancing himself with a hand to Retruance's forward left ear. "What's bad and what's good?"

The Ice Dragon maneuvered alongside, matching wing-strokes with Retruance.

"Indications are it'll snow and turn colder, again," he began. "It's great for me, but some of the less rugged members of the hunt might consider it—well, a bad spell, under the circumstances."

"Constable Dragons are fully capable of staying warm and operative in the worst storms," Tom said. He was never one to let his Companion and his family go undefended.

"Well, of course, boss! I was thinking of the little ones out on the wings? Brought up near the equator, I hear."

"Not to worry!" Furbetrance responded. "We may not like it as well, old Frosted, but we can live through cold weather at its worst!"

Clem glanced at his pocket thermometer and grunted.

"It's dropped fifteen degrees since noon! And the wind has shifted more to the north. We're in for a cold, snowy night."

"Hoarling is right," the Librarian said. "We could lose track, once it starts to blow hard and drift deep.

"But, assuming these new gangsters are locals, what will they do, seeing a storm coming?"

"Bivouac? Burrow down deep somewhere? The horses may be used to cold, but their riders will need to shelter safe," Hoarling insisted. "I should fly ahead and see can I spot their night's camp—while they're still visible!"

"Go on ahead, then," Tom decided. "Take another with you. Flo is our sea-change expert on bad weather. One of the young Dragons can help look and fly back to us with news."

"We must settle to ground, ourselves," Manda added. "No use making things even harder by navigating a blizzard. Furbetrance, you and Hetabelle find us a cave or some sort of shelter for the duration."

The Dragons scattered to their assigned tasks and shortly Furbetrance found, and Hetabelle approved, a tall, dark and thick grove of long-needle pines filling a deep dip among the otherwise grassy hills.

By the time—an hour or more—Hoarling and his party returned, everybody had pitched in to create a cozy and completely hidden campsite. The wind had begun to whistle through the noble pines by the time a cook fire had been laid on a bed of flat stones.

Manda and her pleased assistant Gay began to prepare a hot and savory dinner; Hetabelle and Furbie selected a half-dozen large pines and proceeded to convert their straight trunks into broad planks for a wind-break and a partial roof, while other fragrant bits and pieces were piled neatly nearby for fuel.

"They've camped a bit less than five miles from here," the Ice Dragon reported while the crew awaited dinner to be served. "Place like this, but not as many pines. They know how to go about foul-weather camping. They don't have a wind-breaking barrier, but their hide tents are pitched in a semicircle with backsides to the wind."

"You didn't see Brenda, did you, Ice Monster?" Gay asked eagerly.

"Not exactly, but we're sure she's there. Even in this wind, you can't hide the—aroma—of little girl. I figure she's held in the largest tent—which is good news. These marauders aren't so cruel as to put her in a small tent or out in the cold."

"I should hope not!" cried Gay, shivering in spite of the heat of the fire.

"Everybody get a plate and line up for this roast and some smashed potatoes," Tom called. "Ladies first! Plenty for all—although meat and potatoes are getting a little scarce."

"I smashed the potatoes!" chortled Gay, waving a serving spoon. "Dragon's Delight, Mama called 'em. There's a bit left of the chocolate cake, too, but Mama says we have to clean our plates, first."

"Poor Brenda!" Manda said to Tom, "I wonder what *she* has to eat this dark, cold and stormy night?"

A surprisingly good repast, actually.

For the first time in weeks, Brenda did not have to help prepare meals nor even wash up afterwards. And this food—raw, chopped beef mixed with onions and pickled bits and savory sauces mixed together—was actually welcome to the farm girl who'd been cooking and eating salty bacon, half-baked oatmeal cakes and wormy hardtack aboard a ship at sea.

Not that all was comfort and ease. Far from it! Bouncing along behind a masked rider's saddle for hours and hours was not Brenda's idea of having fun.

When the trooper halted and lifted her down, she ached and pained in places a girl should never feel pain.

The fire, when it at last was burning, was a comfort. You learned to appreciate small blessings, she decided sleepily, in a life like this.

Her rider bundled her into a mound of saddle blankets warmed by hours of being pressed close to horse flesh. She fell asleep in the middle of supper.

Somebody covered her with another warm blanket and lay down beside her to share the warmth.

CHAPTER TWENTY-THREE
The Riders Decide

The substitute Princess awoke at what should have been dawn—but was not, thanks to the raging snowstorm—and climbed out of her cocoon of horse-smelling blankets into the hot, dense atmosphere of the tent.

"Where's the water-closet, if you please?" she asked the guard at the door.

"Closet?" was the guard's reply.

"You know! The latrine! What sailors call 'the head.' Where do we...*uh!* ...relieve ourselves?"

"Oh. Where to go *pee?* Follow the path down to the creek, Princess."

Brenda thanked her and started for the door.

"Wear a coat and put on muffler, mittens, and a warm hat, Princess," the guard warned. "Very cold and blow-y out! You'd freeze solid in a few minutes!"

Although her words sounded coarse, the guard's warning was a kindness, Brenda decided. Perhaps she'd gotten a cold in this weather.

Brenda dug in an inner pocket and found a bit of lozenge someone had given her the day before. She handed this to the girl as she left the tent.

The guard hesitated a moment, then accepted the pastille with a tentative smile.

"Not *poisonous*, is it?"

"No, no! I got it from one of your people. I think she meant well."

The guard waved her through the door, then closed it quickly behind to keep the thick-falling snow from blowing inside.

She popped her hooded head out a second later.

"Keep to the marked path, Princess. Get lost and you may disappear forever—or until springtime, at least."

A half-dozen Black Riders were on the same path for the same purpose, Brenda found. By the time she had found her way back to the tent, she'd discovered what she'd failed to notice during riding the day before.

Every Rider she met or saw was a woman—some young and a few middle-aged!

The very best disguise, Brenda realized, couldn't hide that fact in such circumstances for very long!

The men of *Updraft* hadn't noticed—or knew it and saw nothing unusual about it.

A well-trained, well-armed body of light cavalry!

And all—warriors and officers alike—female!

Brenda snuggled under her blankets and dozed until the duty cooks began breakfast, murmuring softly to each other. One banged an iron pot on the hearthstones and an officer cursed her aloud.

"Damn, girl! Why wake 'em early if we're to stay in quarters until the snow stops?"

"Sorry, Sergeant!" the mess girl answered. "Ready to serve it, anyway, however. Matter of following per—pro—procedures, or rules or orders or...whatever!"

Brenda peeled off her down jacket and leggings and went to the head of the rapidly forming breakfast line without being asked or told.

"Porridge—made with water," announced a cook. "No milk left. No cream for the coffee, either, but we got some brown sugar. You gets it *on* yer porridge *or* in yer coffee. One or t'other. Not both!"

"Porridge with sugar, please. Coffee, I guess. And a piece of that fried bread."

"Bread without butter, for sure," muttered the server. "But there be a bit o' honey left—for officers only."

"I am a prisoner," Brenda reminded her. "I should get honey."

"*Ummm!* Guess a captive Princess gets officer rations."

It was worth playing Princess to get honey, Brenda decided silently. "Thank you, cookie! Knife and spoon?"

"Spoons's what everybody carries," grunted the cook. "Most of us carry our own knifes, too."

"But," Brenda patently pointed out, "I'm your *prisoner*. I have no spoon nor fork nor even a dull knife!"

"Give the Princess a serving spoon," called someone down the line. "Make sure she gives it back!"

"Yessir, ma'am! Baked apple, too, Princess? It's the best part o' break-fast!"

Finding a seat on a chunk of firewood on the other side of the fire, Brenda ate hungrily. She didn't recall being fed the long day before, at all.

She studied her captors more carefully. There were fewer than she had thought. Not half-a-hundred. Not even five and twenty.

More like...fifteen, she decided to herself. *The big soldier-lady with the tall red hat must be their commander. Two others, I see. A half-score of men-at-arms. Rather, women-at-arms.*

She watched the lady with the red hat and, yes, she gave orders and everybody was quick and most respectful, saying "Yes, ma'am," and salut-ing the leader when she called on them to do something.

After breaking fast, things settled down. Most of the troopers returned to their tents to keep warm and dry...and sleep.

Guards were posted at the edge of the grove and, presumably, outside in the swirling snow.

Brenda suddenly moved across the half-circle of tents to approach the officer, who was seated on a camp stool, writing in a notebook.

"Clear off!" warned an armed guard sharply, stepping forward to stop Brenda. "Go back to your tent, at once!"

"I want to speak too your...*Commander*, I suppose she's called."

The Lady in the Red Hat looked up at this and waved at the sentinel.

"Let her come, Fritzi," she said in a pleasant enough voice. "Time for us to get acquainted, now, Princess Gale of Hidden Canyon."

The guard stepped aside and Brenda stepped before the female warrior. "Who are you?"

"Colonel Cobrana, Command of the Free Ride."

The girl was silent for a moment gathering courage to ask, "And who do you say I am, please?"

Cobrana was quite a handsome woman, tall and lean, skin darkened by years of sunlight—although a bit over-muscled, Brenda thought. She had clear, sharp eyes and a manner that reminded the girl of someone she knew; of the Chatelaine of Overhall, Mistress Grumble, strangely enough.

"The Lady Princess Gale of Hidden Canyon Achievement, isn't it?

Over in whatever it's called. *Carolna?*"

"No, I am not, Commander Cobrana! You were told wrong! That awful Captain Downpour lied to you!"

"Which of you should I believe," the lady soldier laughed, "a child—or a sea captain?"

"I am Brenda of Sprend. My father, Augustus Keeper, owns a tavern…"

"You'll have to do better than that, Princess! I know plenty of bar maids and tavern sluts and you don't fit in that disguise."

"I was *chosen* by Princess Royal Alix Amanda Trusslo to be Maid of Honor to her daughter Gale. It's true! Wretched Downdraft stole me on a very dark night in Wall. He thought *I* was Gale."

The Ride Commander leaned back in her camp chair, thinking very hard.

"Have a seat, child. I must carefully consider what you say. I admit you look more like a Maid of Honor than that Downpour ever looked like an honest seaman. Tell me a bit of yourself, then."

"I was born and raised at Babbling Bass Inn in Sprend near Overhall Castle. My parents own and have run the inn for—many a year, Commander."

"And they sold you to be slave to this Princess Gale, *eh?*"

"*No!* I was appointed to be Maid of Honor to Gay—and her friend and companion. The night I was kidnapped, Gay was inside while I went out to catch a breath of fresh air, the breathing was that thick inside."

"But you claim you were raised in just such a place, didn't you? And you had to step outside!"

"My father's Common Room seats no more than twenty or twenty-five on a busiest night of Harvest Time," Brenda said earnestly. "The Tap Room of the Slippery Slope, alone, seated a hundred or more, all rough seamen and tough longshoremen, smoking long clay pipes and thick, sugary cigars and drinking bitter fall ale and stout and flavored gin."

"Ale. My dear child, how much did your father charge for a pint of ale. Can you say?"

"I—don't really know. It changed from season to season. Never more than maybe five cents a mug—with the foam scraped off, ma'am."

The commander nodded thoughtfully, then fished a long, thin, black *cigarillo* from an inner coat pocket.

Brenda bent to pluck a burning splinter from the fire.

"I never saw a lady smoke, before!" She giggled.

"I be a soldier first; woman and lady second and third—and an old fool, fourth," Cobrana laughed ruefully. "I *do* believe you, Brenda of Sprend. And it brings up even more serious problems!"

"Pass me off to your—*uh,* customer? "Brenda asked fearfully. "I want to go home, dear Lady! I can't help you or—or whoever it was wanted poor Gay captured. Carried half-way around world!"

"I tend to agree with you, little Maid, but—we were paid half our fee. And have spent most of it! He will want more than just explanations. He will demand his money back!"

She would say no more but sent her corporal to bring the other Ride officers to her.

Brenda sat silently by her side as the Commander carefully explained the situation to them, ending, "What do you recommend?"

A tall, nervously-thin girl wrapped in white furs and wearing a conical steel helmet, jumped to her feet.

"*I* say—dump 'er in a snowbank at dawn tomorrow and ride out of here, fast!"

"Lieutenant Smock! Your suggestion is refused. We are honorable warriors. Not murderers!"

"If the powerful Satrap Plume learns of *your* mistake, Commander, our whole damn Ride will be thrown naked in the snow! Or, more likely, boiled in oil! We *must* rid ourselves of her, at once, and agree on a story of how she—ran into the blizzard, never to be seen again!"

"*No,* I say! This Ride will not sacrifice an innocent child for a mistake we *all* made," Cobrana growled angrily. "You are a better woman than that, Smock! Your fear has made you an animal! *We* made a mistake. *We* must atone for it to this maiden, her family, and her king!"

"Commander!" said an older woman among the officers. "We must throw ourselves on the mercy of one side or the other."

"We know what kind of mercy the Satrap will show. Recall the hundred wretches chained *upside-down* before his gate?" asked another officer, shaking her head.

The rest nodded, remembering the terrible, horrible sight.

Brenda cleared her throat timidly, leaning forward to look Cobrana in the eyes.

"You may speak, Dame Brenda. You're a part of this problem."

"She's but a child!" Smock protested.

"Problem or solution! She knows the Carolnans we would face. She represents an entire kingdom! Let us hear her!"

"Lord C-C-Commander..." Brenda coughed nervously. "The King of Carolna, the Lord Murdan of Overhall, m'lady the Princess Alix Amanda and her daughter Gale—my very best friend—are all *very* nice people..."

"Nice enough to pardon abduction?" Lieutenant Smock said.

Brenda began to cry but faced Smock through her tears.

"I can't say what they'd do. I'm just a Maid of Honor but I'm as sure as I can be sure of my name, there'd be no awful hanging upside-down."

She fumbled for a dirty, crumpled handkerchief in her pocket and wiped her nose and eyes.

"And I *am* old enough to remember the wicked man called Plume. He was a traitor, a thief, a terrible little sneak and spy! He *ran away* after he failed to throw down poor King Eduard and all his people. My mother told me the stories!"

"When did this happen," Smock, suddenly subdued, asked in a quiet voice.

"Oh, *I* don't know, ma'am!" the little girl wailed. "Ten years ago? No—more like fifteen years. I wasn't even born!"

Commander Cobrana awkwardly patted her shoulder and gave her a clean handkerchief to dry her tears.

"We know a little better, now, and it appears we will be wisest to sue for pardon from Carolna's monarch, this Eduard. And pardon from you, Maid of Honor Brenda. You're a brave lass! You must learn to forgive us and accept our friendship, when things have been explored and explained."

"Oh, ma'am! You've treated me pretty well compared to those nasty pirates. You haven't even made me wash dishes or scrub pans! I'll forgive you—when I get home."

The Commander laughed and her officers joined in.

"Fair enough, Maid of Honor! Now, ladies, we will prepare to ride back east along the Diamond and look for those who might be tracking us. "

"Still snowing hard and drifting," one of her officers reported after peeking through the tent flap. "It'll be hours before the horses can move anywhere at all."

Tom and Clem shoveled down to a bedding of dry pine needles behind the shelter of the sturdy storm fence the Dragons had built to stop the fierce wind.

With the help of Manda and Hetabelle, Byron struggled to erect the tents in the protected ground.

In quick order Hoarling gathered dry boughs and splintered branches, feeding them to Flo, who chopped them to size, arranged them neatly in a conical pile and blew flames on them.

"We'll be safe and sound—and warm—'til the blowing dies down," Tom said, shaking three inches of new-fallen snow from his hood and cape shoulders.

"Doesn't this snow *ever* stop?" Manda asked the Ice Dragon.

"This is mild! Further north snow stays and piles up nicely all year 'round, year after year. Then snow turns to ice. I've seen ice ten thousand feet tick!"

"I stood next to snow on the flat of the Outer Bailey at Overhall," the Princess shivered, "and it was higher than my head! Ten thousand feet—that's almost two miles!"

"And never melts! Very nice and not unpredictable like here in Hintoo."

Tom directed Retruance and Furbetrance to haul a twelve-foot, three-foot-thick log of pitch pine close to the fire.

"Push the middle in the blaze," he said. "It'll catch the fire and burn for at least tonight and all we'll need to do is push the burning ends together, now and then."

"With plenty of nice, bright embers!" Gay approved. "Can we toast marshmallows, Mama?"

"For dessert, child! Clem has bagged us venison for supper. Well, maybe two or three marshmallows now. Dinner will take some time."

Beyond the new barrier, the Woodsman was butchering the slain deer, watched with much interest by the young Dragons.

"*I* could slice it apart with my fore-claws," Charlie Fubetrancedotter told him. "And just as neat, too."

"Now you tell me!" Clem complained. "Well, you can tend the roast and chops on the fire, then. Should be easy for a growing-up Dragonette. We like the meat medium rare. And catch the drippings, dear Chartreuse. A bit of salt and pepper and onion and flour and such? Makes a good gravy."

"When a Woodsman teaches a young Dragon maiden to cook, it's time to find man's work to do." Hoarling snorted in mock disgust. "What say you, Librarian? A bit of reconnoitering about, up along the frozen river?"

"Go ahead, then, Ice Dragon," Tom said with a laugh. "This is your kind of weather. Look and discover but don't be seen if you find these Ride people. They'll be settled down for warmth and comfort as much as we, given this storm."

"Right-o, then, Tom! I'll not be longer than a couple of hours."

"Be back in time for a nice loin roast," Manda called after him.

But he had already disappeared, his silver and blue scales providing perfect camouflage in the storm.

As the afternoon wore on into evening darkness, the Fairy Riders settled down to sleep, sharpen swords, tighten their arrowheads, or play cards on a blanket beside the fire.

Smells of roasting gamecocks began to supplement the aroma of bread, baking to a golden brown before a silvery sheet, which served as a heat reflector.

Brenda shared a large woolen blanket with Commander Cobrana some distance apart from everybody.

At first, these two, Rider Commander and Maid of Honor napped, but then the woman-soldier woke Brenda. . She sat up straight and looked about, blinking in the faint afternoon light.

"Feel like talking a bit?" Cobrana asked softly. "Are you warm enough?"

"Yes, ma'am!"

"Properly said if you were a soldier, I suppose, but I consider you my guest and—I hope—a friend, some day."

" 'Ma'am' is how I was taught to speak polite to ladies," the little girl told her solemnly. "I'd like to use your name, too, however. I think it's a particularly pretty name. Cobrana?"

The Ride officer chuckled softly and tucked the covers around the little girl.

She found a long, brown stick in an inner pocket, bit off one tip, put the *cigarillo* in her mouth and lighted it with a sulfur match.

"You are familiar with smoking tobacco?"

"Oh, yes, ma'am—Cobrana—but I seldom see ladies smoking."

"A habit acquired when I was very young, like you, Brenda, and thought I was so awfully brave and very tough. It's a way of soothing nerves and occupying the hands. I do believe it helps one think."

They sat is silence for a long while, the woman smoking and the child sniffing the tobacco's fragrant smoke and both watching the card game across the way.

"It would help me if you could tell me some things about yourself. And your parents? And those you have met in your short life. You mentioned one Murdan of Overhall? Is the Historian a magician or a wizard?"

"No, *no!* He's...a collector of stories. Of histories. And he also smokes tobacco but in a long clay pipe."

"Remind me to offer him some of this Hintoo Light Leaf. When we meet, I mean. Tell me about him, though. Is he nice?"

"Mostly. He has a terrible temper at times, my father says. My Mama says that hides his good heart!"

"The younger girls of the Ride say much the same about me," laughed the Commander. "And I suppose they're right."

"Mama says there's times to be bright—and times to bellow!"

"I like your Mama, already! If—*when*—we meet I'll tell her that her daughter is quiet, well-behaved, brave, and uncomplaining. What a mother loves to hear of her little girl. I know *my* mother did!"

Cobrana leaned her elbows on her knees and began asking about Tom and Princess Manda—people Brenda felt more comfortable talking about, she saw—and the little girl answered as honestly and simply as she could.

"I just don't know, ma'am," she replied to a question about the number of soldiers at Overhall. "Dozens and dozens, I s'pose. Their leader is Captain Graham. A very nice man, Gay says. She knows him much better than I. I know three or four of his Guards. They came from Sprend. They're grown men, of course. Although Sir Tom calls 'em boys.'"

"You don't have a special boy friend?"

Brenda looked suddenly quite sad. "Yes, but he was on *Updraft* with my kidnappers."

"A pirate?"

"I'm not sure. I suppose. He *was* a crewman on *Updraft*, but he was awfully nice and kind. He did what that grouchy old Captain Downpour and everybody told him. His name is Crippen. Goodness knows where he is now."

Cobrana nodded and smiled a bit wistfully as Brenda described her two friends among the kidnapper's crew, Crippen and the cook everyone called Fats.

"Why 'Fats' I don't know," she added, "for he wasn't fat at all. Not nearly as big as the Captain."

Someone blew three rising notes three times on a horn and everybody stopped what they were doing to line up to heap their tin plates with steaming food.

Cobrana led her charge to the head of the line, saying: "As Ride Commander I get to eat first, while things are still hot. And you, as you are my guest."

Brenda laughed aloud. "Sir Tom says 'R. H. I. P.!' "

"I don't understand."

"It means 'Rank Hath It's Privileges,' Tom says. Kings always come first, then Lords and then Dragons and then such as knights and ladies, you see."

"*Dragons!* The King of Carolna has Dragons?"

The girl shook her head and explained.

"Some people have Dragons as their Companions, you see. Didn't I tell you about that?"

"No, this is news to me, my dear. Here in Hintoo Dragons are very rare. And they're wild beasts! I've never even seen one."

"I've seen a bunch. Tom is Companion of Retruance Constable. Manda is Companion to Furbetrance Constable. And the Lord Murdan I told you about? He's Companion to their father, Gay told me."

"*Three* friendly Dragons! This *is* news to me, Brenda."

"There are several others, m'lady. Furbetrance is married to Hetabelle. They have five littler Dragons. I've never met any of them but Gay knows them."

"Remarkable and *more* remarkable!" Cobrana gasped. "Any more?"

"Let me see. Gay told me about one who lives in the ocean. His name is—*ah*—Flo, or something like that.

"And seems to me there's another named Horrible or Hortense. Or is it Hoarfrost? I really don't remember."

And she fell to devouring strips of soy-marinated beefsteak with fried vegetables and rice.

Everything tasted perfectly delicious.

The bemused Ride Commander ate slowly, thinking of what the child had said. She tucked a sleepy Brenda into a sleeping bag near her own by the fire and wished her "good night."

Smock come into the tent, shaking loose snow from her foul-weather gear and stamping her boots.

Cobrana greeted her. "Is the storm passed, yet, Lieutenant?"

"Much less falling, now, Commander. The wind has died down. I should guess it'll stop before morning. Looks like it added maybe a foot on the level and didn't drift as much as it did last blizzard."

"Pass this word. We'll ride in the morning. Get some sleep, Smock. It won't be easygoing."

Two hundred feet directly overhead, Furbetrance Constable tilted over on his left wing and studied the Ride campsite.

"Where's our little girl, I wonder?" he said to Brazier, just behind him. "Safe enough, I hope."

"Do we attack?" his son asked eagerly.

"Not yet. There're way too many! They might harm Brenda before we could get to her. Look, now! Glide over and settle among those rocks; find a nice hidden place to keep watch. I'll go back and report to Tom. Nothing to do until this snow stops, anyway."

CHAPTER TWENTY-FOUR
Meeting of the Ways

The Ride encampment was astir at dawn. The wind had shifted to the south and already the new banks of snow were shrinking.

The last breakfast had been served and a detail began vigorously scrubbing pots and pans while individual troopers scooped up handfuls of snow and coarse river sand to cleanse their mess kits and utensils.

A trooper led the horses from their shelter. The beasts shook their heads and stamped their hooves, excited by the prospect of action and pleased to be free of the boredom of the two days of waiting.

Each Rider chose the animal she would ride and led those animals chosen for pack duty that day aside to give them a last, careful inspection before they hoisted up and tied heavy packs on their backs.

"I've picked a gentle mare for you," Commander Cobrana told Brenda. "She's run in snow many times and is as sure-footed as a snow marten! Ride beside me. I've decided to take you home."

"Oh, good!" Brenda laughed. "You won't be sorry."

"I do hope not," the lady commander sighed. "It is my clear and present duty, at any rate."

Lieutenant Smock, who stood nearby awaiting orders, protested angrily.

"We owe allegiance to the House of Wang! To the Divine Emperor of Hintoo, Commander! We must take her to…"

"No longer, if there ever was," Cobrana snapped. "It was a wicked and deceitful task, we now know, and not honorable warriors' work! I have decided, Lieutenant. Listen!"

She called her troop about her and spoke in a loud and lordly voice, saying:

"Thus Contract was offered to our Ride by a little, withered man named Plume. I assumed it was offered by the Divine Wang, but I have now learned this was not the case. Our Ride has been an honorable company of warriors since the days of my great-grandmother! Even His Eminence the Emperor could not require us to perform such a despicable task as stealing a mere child from her family! Lieutenant Smock! If anyone disagrees with this, they need only turn in their horses and equipment, pack their personal gear and start *walking* to the Imperial Capital! Decide at once! Those who follow me will go back down our trail seeking forgiveness for our—*m*—mistake! Stand aside, those who choose the traitor Plume! You who agree? We march within the hour!"

Brazier prepared himself to follow the departing horsemen but was disconcerted when the troopers divided into two groups—one large; the other of only five men and these stripped of their weapons and armor and on foot.

"Where…?" he muttered to himself. "Which to follow? Where are Papa and Uncle Retruance?"

The larger group turned east along the river.

"Going off to attack us, I guess. Must warn them! *Ha!* There's little Brenda on that big white mare."

He slipped around a large standing stone and prepared to follow the horsemen downstream toward the Carolnan camp.

"Must warn our guys!" he reminded himself. "But—there's no more cover! Better to fly."

He launched himself in the opposite direction and silently gained enough altitude to hide his bulk in low, light clouds there.

"Papa! *Papa!* Can you hear me?"

Softly but clearly he heard Furbetrance answer—Dragonish *far-calling* he'd heard about but never tried before.

"What say you, Son?"

Brazier quickly described the division of the troop, circling all the while, trying to keep first one and then the other force in sight as they moved further apart.

"We are coning," Furbetrance told him. "Tom says to keep tabs on that smaller group and tell us where they go. It may be some trick!"

"Yes, Papa!"

The young Dragon slid into a stand of cedars nearer the river. The tall, close-set trees let the loose snow slide from their branches at the Dragon's slightest touch. He sternly ignored it falling on his head and cascading down his back, to melt in his body heat and turn to steam.

"They'll see me! They're *bound* to see me!" he hissed to himself.

To gain a view he snaked his neck up and to the right until his right ears and eye were just clear of treetops and the steam.

Beyond the Diamond, he spotted the five soldiers floundering through the wet snow, headed southwest.

Then he softly snorted in surprise.

In the far southwest, he saw a large, grey cloud moving his way. And now he could hear a strange whining rumble—a sort of low, whispering, scraping noise.

And he could hear muffled clops of horses' hooves on hard-packed snow.

"*Papa!* Something awful this way comes!"

"What is it?" his father's voice came.

"Too far yet to see what," Brazier gulped.

"We're on our way. Just watch and report!"

"Retruance and I will meet these bowmen," Tom called to Furbetrance and Clem. "You stay close and wait to see what they have to say."

"I am afraid they're of ill intent," Clem worried. "Who has Brazier seen? Get a closer look?"

"First things first!" Tom said firmly. "That new *whatever-it-is* is still miles away. Come with us, Hoarling, please! Furbetrance? You, Flo and Hetabelle stay with Clem."

Retruance stroked quickly into the clear sky, to perhaps a thousand feet.

"What do *you* think they are intending?" he asked his Companion. "Fight? Escape?"

"One—or the other. We'll see shortly."

Hoarling, some distance ahead and below them, circled back to say, "They've seen us, I think. They've stopped and await us."

"Have they altered formation at all?" Tom wondered.

"Just standing there," the Ice Dragon replied. "Seem to be waiting."

"Do you recognize these fearsome beasties?" Cobrana asked Brenda.

"I—I—I *think* so, Commander. The green one I think is Retruance Constable. His rider—Companion—is Sir Tom. My friend Joy's father. The Librarian of Overhall! Yes! I see Sir Tom on the green Dragon!" A moment later, she added, "I don't know the blue Dragon."

"Looks dangerous, Commander!" said Lieutenant Smock nervously.

"Of course they look that way!" Brenda snapped. "They are Constable Dragons and they are our friends."

"Smock, order the Riders to stand down. The Lady Brenda and I will ride ahead and speak to the Carolnan Knight and his green Dragon."

"Sir, what should I do—if they capture you?"

"That's up to you, Lieutenant. Considering the Dragon alone could probably incinerate the whole troop at a breath, I would recommend you ride away. Fight another day."

"Yessir!" Smock said, frowning.

The Lady Commander and the Lady-in-Waiting urged their horses forward to where Retruance and Tom were already on the ground, watching them approach.

Brazier blew away a thick wisp of steam from below.

"Sill a pair of miles away, Papa."

"Tom and your uncle Retruance are speaking to the kidnappers. Brenda is with them! I sense Retruance is surprised about something. Stand by!"

"I haven't worked this hard *ever!*" Brazier complained. "And all I'm doing is standing still in the snow and waiting!"

"I am Thomas, Librarian of Overhall and Knight of Carolna, Madame Commander. The little maid has told you of me?"

"She has told us and we believe her and who she is, Librarian," Cobrana nodded. "We agreed to meet *Updraft* at Swang Kwo and escort her to our client."

"Who was that? With whom did you make this agreement?"

Brenda spoke before the Commander could answer, "It was that nasty Accountant, Sir Tom! The awful man called Plume who ran away."

"We know Plume all too well, Commander Cobrana. The girl is right. He's not the sort from whom an honest mercenary would accept orders!" Retruance snorted.

"He is a High Minister of the Imperial Government of Hintoo. We didn't know..."

"She *didn't* know," Brenda insisted. "I *like* Commander Cobrana and all her girls. They didn't know! They were good to me! They didn't even make me cook or wash dishes or *anything!*"

"I believe you, Brenda. Commander?"

"Yes, sir!"

"Thank you. I'll send her to my wife. She's not far away. But we...you *and* I...have another problem."

He turned to Retruance and asked, "What does young Brazier have to say?"

His Dragon looked thoughtfully into the bright sun for a minute before he answered.

"They're a mile or two short of the river, he says. He says soldiers are mainly riding in—of all things!—sleighs and dragging toboggans. Drawn by big horses. Heavily armed, he says. Full armor and catapults and such."

Cobrana listened with a worried frown. "It sounds like...Imperials! Nobody else has weaponry like that!"

"We'll have to careful," the Dragon warned. "The Emperor won't like us incinerating his soldiery!"

"A few ideas do occur," Tom said.

He stamped at the turf underfoot, sending up a spray of thin ice, pine needles and mud.

"Here's what we'll do. First: Brenda, Hoarling will take you to Manda. He's not nearly as wicked as he pretends, believe me."

"He looks *really* fierce," Brenda said slowly. "But, then, so does Retruance! Pleased to meet you, Master Hoarling."

"Give her to Manda and come right back to us, Hoarling. I have a very special job for you, m'boy!"

"Something violent and loud, I hope," the Ice Dragon laughed wickedly.

"Bring Furbetrance back with you. Hetabelle will guard the ladies and our camp. If things go wrong..."

The Ice Dragon grinned happily, lowered his great blue head when Clem lifted the little girl to his brow, making sure she could reach Hoarling's foremost right ear.

"Now, here's the drill," the Librarian said to Clem, Retruance and Cobrana.

CHAPTER TWENTY-FIVE
Battle on the Diamond

The battle was sudden, sodden, unexpected—and nearly bloodless. Tom's plan was quite simple.

First, Retruance suddenly appeared before the advancing Hintoo warriors who had just completed their crossing of the frozen Diamond; ten large sleighs each drawn by three heavy-boned draft horses and each crammed with ten men in full armor.

At the appearance of the Dragon, the commanding officer ordered his pike-men to form three ranks facing the beast and companies of archers deployed to their right and left flanks.

As they reached their positions, the archers immediately loosed a flight at the Dragon.

Ignoring their arrows, the tough-scaled Retruance blew a white-hot flame at the ground between himself and the pikers.

The officer ordered an advance of the foot soldiers—just as called for in all Hintoo military manuals.

"The best defense is a strong offense."

But Retruance's blowtorch breath had already melted the snow and ice cover between them, turning the frozen soil to thick, viscous, steaming mud. All three ranks of foot soldiers mired down before they advanced five paces. They were suddenly knee-deep in slippery mud and blinded by steam, as well.

The archers at that point became aware of Furbetrance and Flo behind them on either side, torching the dry brush and tall brown grass.

The Imperial bowmen crowded away from the brush fires into the pike-men and quickly became trapped themselves!

The entire Hintoo company was herded into a smaller and smaller circle of mud surrounded by fire—except to their rear.

Their officers screamed wildly conflicting orders sprinkled with profanity, attempting to separate the bowmen from the spearmen.

Retruance on the northern margin of his boiling mud-puddle, grinned broadly and swatted away the occasional arrow or spear that came his way.

Amidst the terrible tangle, the former Overhall Accountant named Plume seized the commanding Hintoo Colonel by the arm, shouting shrilly, "Back across the river! Set up a new line among those rocks! Do it *now!*"

The Colonel, whose Ancient and Honorable name was Tsu Tsu, nodded understanding but, rather than issue the orders, turned and fled to the river bank, goaded by his own terror.

But where the river had been frozen three feet thick, its water now thundered by at breakneck speed, brown with dirt and filled with ice floes, tumbling and rumbling.

The Hintoo Colonel watched in horror as Furbetrance finished blasting the thick ice on the south margin and then, turning back, saw the Ice Dragon gleefully re-freezing the muck around his floundering soldiers.

Thirty heavy draft horses shrieked in horror and struggled wildly to burst their traces and free themselves of the hot mud.

Infantry and archers, seeing their Colonel advancing to the rear, turned to follow. In a minute the entire Hintoo force was snarled in a shoulder-to-shoulder, back-to-front bewilderment on the flat north bank of the Diamond.

They dropped shields, spears, pikes, bows and swords and fought their way forward on hands and knees, only to reach the river's muddy margin and the rushing water beyond—into which several of their petty officers as well as their Colonel were somehow pushed—or thrown forwards—to be swept downstream.

The wildly furious Plume, afoot on the edge of the mud-hole, screamed hysterical orders and counter-orders after his retreating men.

Hearing horses galloping toward him from the east through the smoke, Plume turned and waved his arms frantically.

"To me! *Help!* Help me!"

Too late he realized the mounted soldiers surrounding him were… women!

"Minister! Stand where you are. You are our prisoner," Cobrana thundered. "Check him for weapons, Smock!"

As he turned to flee, Plume was knocked to the ground by the snarling mash of a large, black dog.

"Haven't seen your ugly mug for a long time, Master Plume! Gone to kidnapping from spying and betraying, I hear. Truss him up well, Riders! He's not to be trusted, *ever.*"

"*Errrrk!*" Plume said—gurgled, actually.

He fainted dead away.

The final act of the almost bloodless victory came when young Brazier, skimming the roaring river, scooped up a sodden, sobbing Colonel Tsu before he could conveniently drown himself.

"Hold on, old boy! I'll warm your fancy uniform and dry you out in a shake or two," Brazier said cheerfully. "Battle is lost and war is cancelled, I would say."

He wrapped the freezing Tsu in his powerful foreclaws and drew him close to his hot breast.

CHAPTER TWENTY-SIX
After the Battle

Tom waved at Retruance as his Dragon circled over the silenced battlefield.

"Come carry this thing back to our camp. Manda'll know what to do with him, and Byron will also, I imagine. Thaw him out and warm and feed him—and we'll carry him back to Lexor for justice!"

"Quicker to drop him in the river," Retruance growled.

"Not my way to do things—nor is it yours, Retruance Constable. I'm surprised!"

"Sorry, Companion! My Dragon dander is up, I s'pose. Will you come with us?"

"No, I want to talk to the Hintoo officer Brazier just fished out of the river. Send him on his way home with a message to his real boss—his Emperor, I suppose. See if we can avoid a war over Plume's plots and ploys."

"Good luck! Bye-the-bye; shall I send word to Eduard? Our rescuing Brenda and capturing Plume, I mean?"

"Secure Plume first. See the ladies are safe and then bring the Tiki to me to speak with the Hintoos."

"And tote some lunch?"

"Yes. I guess we have to feed everybody. The draft horses are scattered all over the flats," Tom nodded. "Commander Cobrana, ma'am? Pick a detail of your prisoners to gather food from the wrecked wagons or all will go hungry."

"Agreed. New camp on higher ground, Sir Thomas?"

The Constable Dragon clapped his wings in a great drum-roll as he rose into the bright noonday sky. He carried the unconscious Accountant in his wide mouth—or he would have shouted in triumph.

CHAPTER TWENTY-SEVEN
Departures

"Are you well?" Tom asked the captive Colonel Tsu.

"I'm a dead man, Sir Thomas! I was defeated. I failed my Emperor!"

"Don't be a complete ass, Tsu! You were the unwitting tool of a very wicked man. A *Human* without loyalty or love to anybody other than himself. Believe me; I know this Plume well.

"Besides, there's no shame in losing a battle to eight Dragons."

The wretched officer let his shoulders sag and he began to weep.

"I was a good soldier, Sir Knight! I did as I was ordered, as best as I could. What must I do, now? What will the Divine One think? What will he say?"

"You'll find out when you get home, Colonel Tsu. I'll give you a letter to show His Most Imperial Majesty when you reach Long-Tsu. I'll try to explain what has happened here and why. If he is a just man, he will understand and forgive. I hope so!"

Disarmed and terrified, the Imperial soldiers were ferried across the raging river by the younger Dragons.

They would have to walk home. Their big draft horses had scattered far and wide. Their bows, swords and spears had been gleefully Dragon-trampled into the mud on the north side of the river.

"Do you think they'll go home to their Divine Emperor?" Clem wondered aloud at supper that night.

"*I* wouldn't!" Manda cried sharply. "Only a Divine Idiot would pass the chance to punish *somebody* for Plume's wickedness."

"I talked a bit to the soldiers." the Tiki said, "and there are some other things to be considered, my dear."

"And they are?"

"The Divine Hintoo Emperor—his name is Monona—is a sickly lad less than twelve years old," Byron explained. "Which is how Plume was able to insinuate himself into royal favor so easily, I imagine."

"And also," he added, "the symbol—the *mascot* you might say—of the Hintoo Emperor *is a Dragon!*"

"This gets too complicated for a simple Carolna lassie!" Gay cried, throwing up her hands.

"Whether Tsu goes home or runs away," Tom soothed her, "we'll be home at Hidden Canyon long before."

"Keep a careful eye on these western lands, I would suggest, Companion," Retruance rumbled from above the far side of the fire. "Somebody pass the tomato sauce—*catch-up*, as you call it for some reason."

The rescue party returned to deserted Swang Kwo where they found the *Updraft* pirates camping in an empty warehouse, hungry and wet and generally miserable.

The cook named Fats greeted them with a rather wary bow. Fats now wore, instead of his old blue denim shirt and a long apron, a peacoat made of sailcloth, badly over-run sea-boots and a short cutlass stuck in his belt.

"Crew voted old Downpour out," he explained. "When the ice floes broke loose, we just barely got ashore before it carried the sloop off downstream—along with the captain, as it turned out. He'd bolted himself in his cabin and didn't hear the warning in time."

"Killed, do you figure?" Clem asked.

"We last saw *Updraft* she was still afloat—or rather, she was being carried off by the moving ice. Sounded like a mill-stone grinding corn! *Maybe* the captain survived—we don't know."

"What do *you* think, then?" Manda asked her husband.

Tom considered a moment, then addressed the marooned sailors.

"Your choice, then. Go home to trial for kidnapping? Or stay here in a deserted ruin—and deal with the Hintoo when they come looking for you.

"What'll it be? Certain and swift justice in Carolna—or make a new life here in Hintoo. Choose!"

A scrawny boy stepped forward, touching his forelock in salute and smiling weakly at Brenda.

"I'll go for King's justice, just to be home again," he said. "I've had more than me fill of these bloody—your pardon, ma'am!—child-stealing tars!"

"This is my friend Crippen!" Brenda said, running to the lad. "I'll speak for him before the King. He's *not* a bad person."

The Librarian nodded soberly, received a nod from his Princess-wife, then turned back to the outlaws.

"Anyone else choose Carolna and King Eduard's law? Last call, now!"

"Come home with us, Fats, dear," Brenda begged. "Papa can always use another good cook in his kitchen—after you've served your term. "

Fats stood, looking uneasily from the Librarian to his sullen mates.

"They need me," he said to the girl. "I'm their chosen leader, now. What'll become of them all, without me?"

Standing next to Gay, Brenda sobbed and grasped her hand, and looked up at Tom, pleadingly.

"What's to become of *you* if you stay here, is the question," Manda put in. "My father is a just man. He'll consider all your circumstances when he rules. I'm as sure of it as—that it's getting on toward evening."

"*Decide,*" Tom said, making himself sound quite stern and certain. *Now!*"

The crewmen shuffled feet, whispered a bit, then moved back into the stone warehouse they had made their barracks without a further word—all of them but the ship's boy and the skinny cook.

"Retruance!" the Librarian called.

"Here, Companion!"

"Gather wood and leave it by the warehouse door. They don't have to freeze for punishment, I guess. Give 'em a haunch of our venison...and a single knife to butcher it with."

"You are *much* too kindly!" Manda objected.

"So we are, then!" Retruance said calmly. "Come help gather a few cords of firewood, Furbetrance. *We* go home tomorrow. *They've* chosen to stay here."

"I'm—I'm—not all that sure," Manda murmured from deep inside their sleeping bag late that night. "They all should be strunk up for a fort-night or two, I say. *Then* hung on a gallows tree! Stealing a little girl! How perfectly awful!"

"*Strung* up. No doubt," her husband yawned mightily. "But, my love, consider! The trial of thirty-four men might take months. We would be called to testify time and time again, and then to consult on verdicts and punishments. Thirty-odd grown men to house and feed and guard day and night. Months of your father's valuable time hearing testimony and pleas! It will be fall before we would get home to Hidden Canyon!"

"Still…" Manda said, propping herself on her left elbow to argue further.

"And remember! There's still the matter of trying and judging Plume as traitor and spy! No avoiding that. To me, *he's* more than a small matter. A Human! How did he get here? And why?"

Manda considered his words in silence.

"You're undoubtedly right—as you almost always are," she sighed at long last. "So be it! I'm going to sleep!"

The Librarian of Overhall, however, was himself already fast asleep.

An hour after midwinter dawn, clear and sharply cold, the Dragon Flight churned into the air with a sound like rolling thunder, formed the customary "V" formation, and followed Retruance Constable toward the rising sun.

"You had all the fun!" Gay complained to her best friend, Lady Brenda of Sprend. They were firmly attached to Furbetrance's rear, right ear, bundled in thick furs and woolen blankets.

"Fun!—if you call freezing near to death, being filthy dirty for weeks on end without a bath? Washing slimy tin dishes and pots and scrubbing scorched pans and kettles without a sliver of soap! Shying from smelly, whiskery sailormen who…well, I don't really *know* what they wanted, but I knew to stay out of their reach!"

"Well, maybe not *fun*. But exciting."

They rode without talking for a while, watching the Diamond roll along seaward beneath them.

"I like *your* young sailor," Gay broke the companionable silence. "What's his name?"

"Crippen? Crippen Aldershot is his full name. He's a poor country boy from a tiny village near Morningside. He hated herding goats so he ran away to sea when he was twelve."

"Seems very nice, if a bit rough around the edges," Gay told her, but Brenda was leaning over the side of Furbie's right cheekbone, trying to spot the coastline of Hintoo.

"*I'll* have some exciting adventures, myself, some day," Princess Gale of Hidden Canyon added to herself.

And she wriggled deeper into the fur comforter as Dragon Flight began to climb over a bank of thick grey clouds shrouding the coast.

CHAPTER TWENTY-EIGHT
Preparations for a Trial

Overhall's wizard-in-residence looked up at the sound of tapping on the stained-glass center window of the Historian's library.

" 'Tis your Dragon," Arcolas called to Murdan, deep in the back stacks of books, pamphlets, manuscripts, notebooks, scribbled-on napkins and slips of foolscap at the far end of the large room.

Arbitrance Constable perched precariously on the balcony but managed to thrust his vast blue head into the room, accompanied by a cold blast of wind.

"Coming!" the Historian called from his cluttered recess. "Welcome back, old lizard! Get him something to drink or eat or both, Arcolas, me lad."

"He sounds rather pleased with something," Arbitrance chuckled. "Have them bring me something hot and ready to drink, Wiz. I may not mind cold but I really don't care for it, at all. Where's the King? Not here?"

"With his troops across the way," Arcolas answered. "His Majesty feels he owes it to his men, I gather, to share their discomforts in the field, as it were."

"I said to him," Murdan told them, dropping a dusty pile of books on the floor by his desk, "plenty of spare room in Overhall! He would be more comfortable under cover."

"That's not Eduard's style of general-ing," the Dragon insisted. "Share the chilblains, eh?"

"Tell me about the road to the east," Murdan demanded. "When will it be passable?"

"No problem even now, as far as that goes," the Dragon said. "It greatly improves as you travel toward Lexor."

"This wind promises warmer blowing by tomorrow midday," the Magus told them. "You and the King have kept the troops days longer than ever before, except during officially declared warfare. It just isn't healthy, m'lord, to keep so many men in flimsy tents in winter."

Arbitrance laughed. "No fears! Tom says the invasion we feared never existed. The snowstorms were natural, *not* magical! They've recovered little Brenda, safe and sound, and dealt with the culprits—mainly our old enemy, Plume!"

"Great! Good tidings!" his listeners cheered.

"I'll pass word to Eduard and Ffallmar to begin mustering-out, now the road is clear enough for soldiers."

"I think, m'lord, we all deserve a good night's sleep, now," Arcolas said.

"You're right, as you often are—although I hate to admit it, Magician."

He sent Arbitrance flying off to invite the King to dinner. "I suppose I should throw a feast and let Eduard give out medals and such things."

"Dame Frabble is planning a gala victory feast," Arcolas said. "She knows you well, Lord!"

"Go you help her plan, then," growled Murdan. He felt a bit jealous about the way his underlings seemed to know him so well.

Harboring bright visions of lemon sponge cake and chocolate-filled cookies, not to forget huge beeves roasted for hours over an open pit of hardwood coals in Outer Bailey—enough to feed a small army—Arcolas sped happily off to the kitchen.

"My older son says more, Companion," his Dragon added as he carefully prepared to withdraw from the window. "They're coming to Wall, just now, to bring home Clem's brother and his shipwrecked sailors. Tom plans to reach Overhall on Sunday."

"That sets the day and time for a Victory Feast, then," Murdan decided. "Anything else?"

"They bring the captive Plume with them. Something to discuss with the King."

"Trial of the century! More so even than the Gantrell trial. Ask Eduard to bring Graham with him. We'll get an early start on arrangements."

Arbitrance nodded and released his claw-hold on the balcony rail, dropping headlong toward the cobbles below.

At the last possible moment, he snapped his wings out with a sound like a thunderclap, lifted his great head and shot like a cannonball straight through the open gate, crossed the Gugglerun draw, and plunged down the slope toward the encamped Army of Carolna.

CHAPTER TWENTY-NINE
Discussions and Decisions

Tom shook his head and frowned fiercely at his employer.

"He's clever! He's wickedly devious! He's evil to the bone! He's smart enough to be prepared and you can bet he's prepared to beat the rap, somehow."

"He's *Human,* isn't he?"

"Are all Elves pure? How about Gantrell?"

"Well, there *are* wicked…" Murdan coughed.

"Exactly! And everywhere! There were high-placed thieves even at the Library of Congress! And some were Congressmen and even Senators!"

"D'you two plan to make a point to this?" asked Manda. "I say we put him to sleep until the trial starts. And hang him soon after!"

"No, sweetheart! I won't agree to that! Only the most able physician could keep him safely asleep for days or weeks."

"Arcolas is highly qualified," Manda insisted. "We could trust him to take good care of Plume…don't you think?"

"I wouldn't put that sort of—of—*responsibility* on poor old Arcolas. Let me ask you, Historian: Who suffered most from Plume's lying and cheating?"

"Manda."

"My wife? Mother of my child? Princess of Carolna! You'd make her a jailor?"

"Leave him to me, though," Manda growled again.

"I—I—" Now it was Tom who coughed, uncertainly.

"*Ah*—I've a better idea," came Retruance's deep voice from the open window. "Furbetrance!"

"My Mount? A Dragon? I don't think that would be legal, Retruance," Manda snapped angrily. "Dragons aren't...citizens, or something."

"That's news to me," the Librarian said in surprise. "I assumed..."

"We've always been welcome guests of the Crown, Tom," Retruance explained. "Old Eduard Eighth, our Eduard's grandfather, said so. Constable Dragons were so honored—and are still."

"Manda's great-grandfather? I never heard that."

"It's true!" Murdan nodded, waving a hand toward the Dragon. "He's right. My father wrote the proclamation!"

Retruance lowered his massive chin to a brightly-patterned rug spread below the window.

"Accused can name *anyone* to defend himself he wants—within reason. Including himself!

"Yes, Dragons are not citizens, subjects, vassals or slaves to anyone, anywhere. We are welcome visitors, playmates, teachers, allies, guardians, guides, social and political advisors, and friends. Occasionally we are Companions to special people of our own choice.

"We can even be lawyers, if need be."

"Well said! All agreed?" The Historian ended the discussion. "But—will Arbitrance take Plume's case?"

"Will Plume accept Arbitrance as councilor?" Tom added.

"Accused has the right to his own choice in that matter," Murdan told them. "But the Court can appoint an attorney as advisor, if Accused decides to represent himself."

"I'll go ask Furbie immediately, then," Manda declared, rising from her seat. "Go on without me, please."

The members of the hearing stood as she left.

"Sit down!" Murdan rapped his desk top for order. "You also, please, Eduard."

"This is your Achievement and your duty," the King said softly. "What's next?"

"The structure of the Royal Court. The King serves as or appoints a Royal Magistrate. Accused may ask for a jury trial—but I don't think this one will. He will think he will be better served, I should think, by a trial before you alone, Eduard."

"I will serve as Royal Magistrate," the King agreed.

Arcolas, who served as Scribe to the preliminary hearing, wrote furiously, taking down the words that flowed back and forth.

Tom went looking for his princess/wife and found her and Gay sitting in the sun on the stone curbing of the well above Outer Bailey.

"Child, you may *not* throw pebbles in the well water," Manda was saying when he joined them. "Here's your Papa! Maybe he'll take you to the drawbridge so you can fill the moat with your stones, dear. I'm sure the Man-O-War jellies won't complain. They probably get lonely, being covered with ice much of the winter."

"Oh, *will* you take me, Papa?" Gay chirped. "O' course, I'*m old enough* to go alone, but I want someone to carry a lot of stones. This jumper has not much of deep pockets…"

Tom sent her ahead, promising to come to her in a few minutes. "Your beautiful Mama needs to hear the outcome of Lord Historian's meeting.

"And how did Furbetrance take it, then?" he asked Manda when he was seated beside her on the curbing.

"He rumbled, grumbled, groaned, roared and spat—spitted?—foul-smelling vapors, but he agreed. He will serve. And do well, I think."

"Good old Furbie!"

"But, with a preservation…"

"Reservation?"

"Whatever! He wants you to go with him to interview the Accountant. At least the first time, this afternoon."

"Is he afraid of Plume?"

"No, not *afraid*. He said something about wanting a Human on hand, just in case."

"Probably not a bad idea. I'll go along and maybe calm old Plume down a bit. He's done a lot of wild raving and foul talk, I'm told."

"Let 'im rave, says I!" Manda snapped. "It won't serve him, at all! Now tell me everything said after I left."

"A lot, but it boils down to this: Your father will preside. Murdan will lead the prosecution. Graham is bid most sternly to hold the prisoner close and safe, but with as much gentleness as Plume will allow.

"Eduard will name four Justices to assist him, as needed. He didn't name them. Two each from Small Achievements and Great Achievements. Murdan suggested he appoint Ffallmar as one of the former. And your Uncle Granger for one of the latter."

"Good choices, I should say."

"And you and I—and several others immediately involved in the Plume affair will be free of official Court duties. But we can't go home until this matter's decided, dearest."

Manda sighed. "We expected that, didn't we?

"Let me see! Trial will begin here at Overhall on the First of April..."

"April Foolishness Day!"

"Murdan says that's quite appropriate. Always a lot of foolishnesses to cover when a trial begins."

"Ah, that's me Uncle Murdan! I suppose he's right, though. Sweetheart! Go rescue your daughter from sea urchins and sand dabs in his moat. Then go talk to Furbie and his client."

The former Accountant of Overhall had been placed under heavy guard in the same tower cell from which he had escaped some years earlier.

The round tower-top chamber was small but clean, warm and comfortably, if sparsely, furnished.

Plume was chained by his left ankle to an eye-bolt in the middle of the floor, a heavy chain just long enough to allow him to lay a-bed, sit at a small iron table bolted to the stone floor, or stand at the single barred window overlooking the rushing moat, fifty feet below.

"May we speak to you, Master Plume, sir?" Furbetrance inquired politely from the window.

Plume jerked around, swearing foul words Tom hadn't heard since he was in college.

"Get away, you freaking, foul, misbegotten, slimy reptile! Leave me alone! Go to...!"

The Dragon, that could have turned the prisoner to a soggy pile of sizzling cinders where he stood, explained calmly over the shrill curses, "I am Furbetrance Constable. I am appointed by His Majesty King Eduard of Carolna to be your legal counsel."

"Eduard'll never railroad me that way," the Accountant sneered. "I will act as my own attorney..."

Tom had climbed the eight flights of stairs to the tower-top room, unlocked the door and entered, locking the heavy door behind, leaving the four Overhall Guardsmen outside.

"Defendant who serves as his own attorney has a fool for a lawyer!"

Clarence Darrow said it, perhaps? Or Oliver Wendell Holmes?"

"You! Filthy traitor to our race! Enemy! You—"

"Sit down and shut up long enough to get your defense going. Your Attorney-of-Record is the good Dragon at your window. He *will* serve, whether you like it—or him—or not."

The older Human threw up his arms and howled, calling Tom several ancient Anglo-American gutter words.

"We need some calm, here, I see," Furbetrance snorted angrily and he shot out a thin, red jet of flame at Plume's ankle chain.

Now the Accountant howled in fear, "Torture! Deadly bullying!" and rolled on the floor, trying to free himself from the heated iron.

"Sit!" the Dragon sharply ordered.

Plume whined for mercy but clambered quickly onto the cell's single stool.

Tom shook his head reprovingly at the Dragon and emptied the water jug on the heated chain.

"I am here, as you can now see, to protect you from this Dragon's very hot anger if you don't behave. Don't tempt fate! You are accused of high treason and espionage. Both are capital offenses under Carolna law. Here a King's word is unchallengeable! There's no appeal!"

"D-d-d-death if I'm convicted?" asked the Accountant, now weeping.

"Does that surprise you, Plume?"

"I plan to ask mercy because of your 'disturbed mental state.' And other things," Furbie told Plume.

"Never! Insanity? I'm as sane as your silly King himself, believe me. Saner, perhaps!"

"Usual sentence for 'diminished mental capacity,' or whatever the Court calls it, is to be marooned on a lost island somewhere with a selection of seeds, a stone hatchet, a wooden shovel, and a barrel of fresh water, so I've read. For the remainder of your life."

The prisoner keened and sobbed and hit his head on the iron tabletop.

"Good! Now you understand where you are, Master Client. Wear out with this foolishness and listen to Tom. He has some ideas that might be useful."

"I am lost! I am dead! I am condemned even before I am tried!" Plume choked.

The Dragon and the Librarian let his loud sobs die away to pitiful hiccups before Tom said, "I need some information. Will you answer my questions, old man? Truthfully? Your very life depends on you telling me

156 • Don Callander

what I need to know."

"Ask, then, Thomas Whitehead! I have no reason to lie."

The prisoner hauled a dirty handkerchief from his hip pocket and swabbed his face of tears and smudge.

Tom and the Dragon waited silently.

CHAPTER THIRTY
Trial

Manda took Gay and Brenda to visit Brenda's folks in nearby Sprend where they ran a sturdy, comfortable, busy inn called The Babbling Bass.

The little girls gleefully swarmed over everything from the cobblestone courtyard with its well-cared-for horse-stalls, to the dusty barnyard with contented cows, wooly yews—and a great and fearsome bull in his pen.

They excitedly scrambled to the top of the quarter-full hayloft and threw themselves down into deep piles of sweet-smelling hay, screaming with delighted fear and frightening the brown hens roosting in the chicken yard.

"And the food is wonderful!" cried Princess Royal Gale of Hidden Canyon, "Better'n the cooking at Overhall!"

"Not nearly as good, *I* say," argued Brenda.

It was as close to a disagreement as the friends ever got.

Manda sat in the sun on a small terrace overlooking the noisy little stream with Brenda's mother Susan and Brenda's father, the impressively huge Innkeeper Augustus.

They drank Hintoo's best black tea, and Manda told the keeper and his jolly wife things they couldn't have heard about the adventures of the kidnappers and the Fairy Ride.

"They already sound like chilly night tales," laughed Augustus, " 'though I know all too well they're true."

Manda nodded soberly, patted Susan on the arm, and asked for a second cup of the delicious tea.

"And did the hard winter weather harm your business, Master Augustus?" she asked.

"Not *too* badly, Princess. Business was poor for a long while, but even the deep snow didn't stop our regulars; thank goodness! We're used to cold and snow from long ago. I remember one year…"

Murdan made short work of preparing to prosecute Plume—he turned the work of gathering evidence and lining up witnesses to Tom and his staff and to Arcolas.

He read what they put before him, nursed a spring head cold, and refrained from firing Arcolas because he needed him more as a Wizard (at which he was very good) than as a physician (at which he was pretty good, but not good enough to cure a head cold) and tried to heed his advice.

"Get plenty of rest. Drink lots of liquids. Your cold will be cured completely in two weeks," Arcolas promised.

"And if I don't?"

"Cold will cure itself in a fortnight," the Magus said and quickly changed the subject.

The King stayed with his troops at Overhall until the roads east were cleared for travel, then he returned to Lexor. There was a backlog of kingly business to attend to at the capital.

Queen Beatrix and their twins Amelia and Ednol traveled up from the southland to join him. They would all return to Overhall for the *Trial of the Century*, as the gossips and the town criers called it.

Most of the Dragons went their own ways—Hetabelle and her children to their rookery on an island at the mouth of the Cristol in the far west. The Ice Dragon stayed in northern Hintoo, keeping an eye on things in the uneasy Empire, ruled by a very young boy.

Furbetrance and Altruance stayed close to Overhall.

Clem flew off on Arbitrance to bring his Mornie and their boys to Overhall, all three brown as berries and healthy as horses.

Most of the Volunteer Army were released to their homes, although several dozen asked permission to camp near Overhall. Murdan thought it was a great idea—and placed them under command of Lieutenant Greysolon to be an honor guard and traffic police as crowds began to gather to witness the trial.

Eduard Ten rapped firmly on the desk before him with a wooden mallet borrowed from the Overhall master carpenter.

"This Court Royal is called to order. We will hear charges of espionage and abduction and other crimes against the Common Law of Carolna.

"Please all be seated. Remember that spectator applause *or* condemnation are strictly forbidden. Offenders, after being warned the first time, may be removed from the courtroom *and* the castle by Bailiff and charged with disturbing the King's Peace.

"Bailiff, open the windows. It's going to get hot in here very shortly."

After a few moments of rustle and confused whispering, bringing a warning rap of the gavel, the Great Hall of Overhall Castle fell silent.

Four Guardsmen in full regalia and with drawn swords led the unfettered Accused into the courtroom.

Plume slumped into his seat facing the King. He looked neither left nor right, nor did he meet anyone's gaze.

After a few more moments of rustle and murmur, the courtroom fell silent again.

"Accused, state your full name, please," Eduard directed.

"I am Robert Early Plume."

"You will address the Court as 'Your Lordship,' " the Clerk of the Court warned Plume severely.

"Sorry, Your Lordship. I am unfamiliar with the…"

"Accepted," Eduard interrupted. "State your occupation or profession, please."

Plume answered in a low voice. He was a Certified Accountant.

"Speak so all may hear, please," Court Clerk said.

"Yessir, your Lordship."

"I am *not* a Lord," protested the Clerk.

"Let it go, Master Clerk," the King sighed. "Accused will speak loudly enough for all to hear. Do you understand me, Master Plume?"

"Yessir. Yes, Your Lordship."

"Good enough. Now Master Plume, tell us your place of your birth."

"I was born in Brawley in the State of California in the United States of America, your Lordship."

Murmurs swelled up again at this, but Eduard waved his gavel at the spectators and they fell still.

"The Clerk will read the charges brought against Accused by the Crown."

"Yessir. Yes!" piped Plume, cheerfully.

Clerk opened his mouth to protest again, but a frown from the Bench stopped him short. "Court will instruct Accused *as necessary*, myself, Master Clerk!"

"Yessir! I mean—yes, m'lord."

The Clerk shuffled a thick sheaf of closely written papers and began to read aloud. The charges numbered twelve, but basically added up to the two: *espionage* and *abduction*.

"How do you plead to the first charge?" asked the King.

"Not guilty, Your Honor."

Clerk swallowed angrily but said nothing. The King went through the entire list and received the same answer to each.

Eduard glanced at the clock on the wall behind him. It was a few minutes 'til noon.

"Crown Attorney will next be asked to present his case, I suppose, but—as I assume it will take some time—we'd better recess for lunch?"

"No objection, m'lord!" said Murdan, bowing to the Bench.

"No objection what-so-ever, Your Lordship!" Furbetrance said.

"Well, *I* object! Let's get this farce over and done," Plume growled.

"Overruled," Eduard said calmly. "Court is adjourned for lunch. The gavel goes down to resume promptly at two o'clock."

Manda hailed Tom and Clem at the door. Mornie accompanied her and they carried a large wicker basket between them covered with a red-and-white checkered cloth.

"As predicted, not much action this early in a trial," Tom said, taking the basket. "A picnic?"

"You should see the waiting line outside Dining Hall. Ask Retruance to take us to a quiet, grassy hilltop somewhere—dry and sunny and not too breezy—for lunch. We've infected our daughter and Mornie's boys on

Brenda's family for the afternoon."

"*Inflicted,*" Tom corrected her.

The first witness for the prosecution was Graham, Captain of the Overhall Guard. He described how a heavily armed company, known as Mercenary Knights, was admitted by Accused to Overhall Castle during the Lord Historian's absence.

He testified their leader, one Basilicae of Plaingirt, had admitted to him, later on, the purpose of the attack had been to carry off Princess Royal Alix Amanda Trusslo.

"His statement was taken down, signed, notarized and made a part of the Overhall Castle record," the soldier said. "I have it here in my hand."

"Pass it to Clerk of Court," Eduard ordered, "to be a part of the record of this trial. Do you have questions for Captain Graham, Defense?"

Plume opened his mouth, looked up at Furbetrance, and shut it with a loud snap.

"We have no questions at this time, m'lord," Furbie said.

Eduard nodded to Clerk who nodded to Murdan. He cleared his throat and said, "Call Sir Thomas of Overhall, Consort to Princess Alix Amanda Trusslo, father of Princess Gale of Hidden Canyon Achievement and..."

"That will do," the Court interrupted. "Everybody knows Tom."

He smothered a grin behind his hand. "Prosecutor, if you insist on giving full introductions to *everybody* we'll be here for a year!"

"First, m'boy, tell the Court where *you* were born and how you came to Carolna and accepted employment here at Overhall."

"I object! Question is irrelevant and immaterial!" rumbled Furbetrance, who was obviously enjoying being defense attorney.

"Overruled," decided the Court.

Tom testified about his birth in the United States of America, his employment as a librarian, and how he had been mysteriously transported to Carolna from a subway station in Washington.

The spectators were perplexed by the strange terms and wanted to talk about them. The Court tapped his gavel.

"You magically cause this transportation to Carolna?" Murdan asked.

"No, sir! I was not then and am not now in any way adept at magic."

Tom briefly described his meeting Princess Manda, and his rescue of her from captivity by her ambitious uncle, Lord Peter of Gantrell.

The spectators, all of who knew Tom's story as well as they knew their own, applauded enthusiastically until the Court threatened to clear the courtroom.

"At what point did you realize Accused was spy and agent of the Lord of Gantrell?" Murdan asked.

"We—you and I—discovered his part when he arranged the abduction of my wife on her way to Lexor. His motive was to place Peter of Gantrell on the throne of Carolna through removal of Eduard Ten and of Manda, who was at that time his only heir. When King Eduard remarried and his second Queen bore him a male heir, Prince Ednol, Plume enchanted Altruance Constable to abduct the baby Prince. From this it became clear the Accountant's role was *not* that of Gantrell's lowly tool but that of the prime plotter!"

"And how do you know this to be true?"

"It was admitted before a number of witnesses by Peter, himself. And because Plume, when placed under arrest for plotting against the King, the Royal Family, and the Realm, fled beyond our borders to avoid trial."

The five days that followed brought testimony by Manda, by Clem of Broken Land and his wife Mornie, by several Overhall servants, soldiers, advisors and Ffallmar, and the reading of sworn testimonials by Retruance, Furbetrance and their father Arbitrance, concerning their parts in the matter of the abductions of Princess Manda and of her step-brother, Ednol.

On the sixth day, the Court called the lead attorneys to the bench.

"I don't know about you or the Accused, but the Court is exhausted. Unless either of you can present a really good reason not, the Court intends to adjourn for the weekend."

Murdan and Furbie exchanged glances and then both turned to look toward the sagging figure of Accused.

"I will insist on it," the Dragon said. "My client looks *like death warmed over,* as Tom says."

"The Court looks rather ragged, too," admitted the Historian. "I will not object to a recess until Monday, Eduard. Tom pleads, however, for a few minutes to speak to you in chambers. If it please the Lord Justice?"

Eduard sighed—another of a number he'd uttered quietly since the trial began—and nodded.

"I'll grant him a few minutes. Then I'm going to take a long nap and go out in the sun and play ball with my twins."

CHAPTER THIRTY-ONE
The Defense of Plume

Tom knocked on the door to Eduard's suite and entered when he heard his father-in-law call, "Come!"

Eduard sat in his bed holding a steaming cup of tea. Pretty Queen Beatrix perched on the side of the bed, working stitches into a large square of fine crewel canvas.

"You need some relaxation," Tom apologized, "but I have an idea, I think. And it'll give you the weekend to think it over before trial resumes."

"Of course, Tom! Will you excuse us a while, my dear?"

"No, please don't go, Beatrix. This won't take long and I'm sure you'll have good advice for us both."

Eduard and Beatrix listened at first out of curiosity, but soon Tom saw their interest grow.

"It sounds right," said Beatrix, putting down her needlework. "Are you sure it would be suitable? It sounds *too* good."

"Consider the alternatives, Mother. Murdan, who's far from squeamish in such matters, says the Court has two other choices: life in prison—or death by hanging," her husband said slowly. "We haven't hung—*hanged*—a convict in Carolna in more than twenty years…"

"But—couldn't he return? He came back once before, didn't he?"

"No, not really, Mistress," Tom answered. "Arcolas assures me such a *transposition*, as he calls it, requires *enormous* spelling power. Tremendous effort of magic by a Master Wizard!"

Eduard swung his legs over the edge of his bed and stood.

"What I need to know is: how did it happen to bring him—bring *both* of you—to us. And who spelled it?"

"The Tiki has theories, but even he doesn't know for sure. Most likely the late Emperor of Hintoo, an insanely wicked and extremely powerful Wizard! And he did it for purposes *completely unrelated* to Carolna."

"And that terrible Wizard is gone? Dead?" Beatrix shivered at the thought when Tom nodded.

"It's worth considering," Eduard decided. "I must talk to Byron Bold-face, myself. It'll take weeks to get him here, I suppose...?"

Tom grinned broadly.

"Byron is *here!* He's gone trout fishing near Sprend."

"Let's get a little sleep and a good breakfast," Eduard told him. "Then we'll join the good Tiki. Tomorrow morning. Early!"

"What does this mean, however?" Eduard asked, shaking his head. "The old Emperor was long dead you say, Tiki. Plume is guilty of his crimes on his own hook. Especially the abduction of my children. He deserves to die for that alone, if not for the espionage. Why in all Tunkett can't people play these games by *civilized* rules?"

"The damage was done, dear Sire. Many harms and deaths of soldiers and seamen and innocents were a direct result of Plume's plots, plans and actions," the Tiki murmured softly and sadly. "You—*we*—cannot let him go unpunished!"

Eduard nodded unhappily.

"And it devolves upon me, both as the harmed parent and as Sovereign ruling Carolna, to make the decision. You both have been very helpful, Tom and Byron. Now I must have time to consider what's to be done and decided in my Court."

"I would do it for you if I could, you know," Tom said, embracing his father-in-law.

"The top is a lonely perch, many times," Eduard admitted ruefully.

It was a long, *long* weekend.

Time oozed by more slowly than Tom had ever known it, before. The weather improved until it was almost summer on the walls of Overall Castle.

"We should go down and spend some time with the girls," Manda said.

"Sit on the inn porch and drink lemonade. Talk about nothing special with the Innkeeper and his wife."

"So we shall," Tom agreed. "It's a bit too far to walk. Shall I call Retruance?"

"No, please, let's go on horseback," the Princess said. "I want to see the warming earth putting forth those little white flowers and the last of the ice melting alongside Gugglerun."

"Daffodils, too, I think," Tom said as they rode down from Main Gate to the stream. "Always have been my favorite flowers!"

"I like lilacs, best," his wife said.

"Well, yes, lilacs. White and red and blue and purple…but the little white flowers? What are they called? I forget!"

"*Baby's Breath,* I think."

"No, I don't think… Remind me to look them up, when we get home."

"Retruance will know. He knows all about plants and flowers."

They talked flowers and remembered the deep drifts that blocked the roadway only a few weeks earlier.

They avoided anything concerning the trial.

But the trial of Plume was in their minds all weekend.

Furbetrance Constable cleared his throat—a long, low, apologetic thunder—and addressed the Court.

"If it please the Court, I call Captain of the Guard Graham."

"Captain Graham, please take the stand," the Court directed. "You are still under oath, Captain. You may proceed, Attorney for Defense."

The Dragon nodded his thanks and turned to the soldier.

"When Overhall was occupied by the Mercenary Knights under Sir Basilicae of Plaingirt, as you have testified, where were *you,* Captain?"

"I was serving Lord Murdan in Lexor, where he attended Spring Sessions, sir."

"So, you did not witness the attack, personally."

"That is correct, sir. When I returned here, they were already in full possession."

"And tell us, how did you learn the news of this armed invasion. Who told you?"

"I was informed by my Lord Murdan."

"And how did Lord Murdan learn of it?"

"I really don't know, sir. I assumed somebody sent him a message from here or from the neighborhood."

"You *assumed?* He didn't tell you?"

"No, sir."

"And you didn't ask?"

"That's right. There wasn't time for idle chit-chat. We left Lexor for Overhall within the hour."

"So, as far as you know, what you heard was hearsay?"

"No, Dragon! What I heard was an order from my master to decamp at once and return to Overhall! I obeyed."

"Ah, I see. Let me ask you one other question, Captain. When the castle had been retaken, did you receive orders to arrest Accountant Plume?"

Graham took a deep breath and sat up straighter, striving to appear calm.

"No such order was given. We—the Lord Historian and I—questioned Basilicae for some time. He never said Plume had anything to do with the sneak-in."

"Then when *did* you find out about the *possible* involvement of the Accountant in the taking of Overhall?"

"*Ah*—I believe Lord Murdan told me. Yes, that was after Princess Manda's party was attacked on the north shore of Lakeheart Lake. By armed men from Lord Gantrell's Overtide."

"Still, who told you the capture of a Princess Royal was the doing of my client?"

"Now, that was Gantrell, himself, after we finally arrested him—in Lexor," said Graham, with a sigh.

"And you—and the Lord Historian and Librarian Thomas—believed him?"

"Well, Plume was the only one who *could* have known where Princess Manda would be at the time!"

"My Lord," Furbetrance said, turning to the Bench, "I submit this testimony *proves* nobody believed my client was a part of a conspiracy to carry off the Princess or the little Crown Prince."

"I suppose you are correct as far as you've gone," Eduard told him. "But you must now look beyond the North Shore…"

Over the following three days, Furbetrance meticulously and methodically examined twelve witnesses, from Manda to the soldiers who guarded the Accountant while he was originally imprisoned atop Aftertower.

"*Nobody,*" the Dragon said, tapping the floor with his sharp, right foreclaw, "at *any time* saw or heard or read of Master Plume participating in, directing, or even just planning the crimes of which he has been accused.

"I put it to you, Sire! In a case this serious should not the Court *insist* on something more substantial than hearsay?"

"I ask *you*, Furbetrance—are you finished with your defense? Or will you present further evidence and counter-arguments?"

The Dragon shook his great head slowly. "I have done my very best and all, your Lordship."

"And you have done extremely well, my friend. This Court will now retire to consider the evidence. I will deliver my decisions and render justice in each case—as soon as possible."

"M'lord!" cried Plume, jumping to his feet. "I humbly petition the Court to grant me parole. I respectfully remind the Court that any accused is *innocent* until the Court renders decisions."

The Great Ballroom was completely hushed, waiting once more.

King Eduard Tenth tapped his gavel thrice, softly.

"Petition is denied. Accused will be returned to his cell under careful guard until Court is prepared to announce decision on each charge.

"Court is adjourned."

CHAPTER THIRTY-TWO
Decision of the Court

Thursday morning dawned sunny but cool and windy.

"It'll rain before eleven," Tom predicted. "I hear mutters of thunder in the northwest!"

"I plan to collect Gay and bring her and Brenda back to Overhall," his wife said, drawing on a long wool sweater and bending to pick up her umbrella. "Furbie is looking for some outdoor exercise and I told him he can go with us to Canyon House as soon as Papa decides."

"Poor Papa! Beatrix wants to take him to Knollwater. He needs a few days in the sun—and the warm rain—with his family before Spring Sessions begins."

"You are the world's most terrific son-in-law, beloved! Come with me to Sprend? We should be back after lunch."

"I would, but the King has sent word he will want me and Murdan to wait upon him before noon."

"If I didn't know it's important," Manda sighed, tying her sun hat under her chin, "I would be angry with him. Give him a hug for us, Tom. He needs all such loving he can get, Beatrix says."

Clem and his boys trudged down the grassy slope to the river, with a joyous Blackly Barquest, the Ramhold herding dog, dashing first right, then left, barking at the top of his considerable voice and pausing only to sniff at rabbit holes and aromatic droppings of cattle and goats.

"Spring is here, officially," Clem said to the boys and the dog. "Time we started retting up our gear for winter trapping, now."

"Mama isn't feeling well," young Thomas said, a worried frown marring his normally sunny face.

"Mama," his older brother Gregor smiled confidently, "is 'with child!'"

"You're thinking of Aunty Manda," Thomas Clemsson snorted. "Mama'd've told me!"

"When you reach a *certain age*," Gregor said in that superior tone of older brothers, "you get to noticing such things."

"*What* things?"

"I'll tell you. Some day," Gregor giggled.

"Mama *is* pregnant, too. She wanted to tell you herself. She will deliver a baby in—*oh*—about four months," Clem told his sons. "Greg's right—and I'll make him tell us both *how* he knows. But not *here* and not *today,*"

"*I* should know, if *he* knows," sniffed the boy. "*Oh, look!* Ol' Blackly has chased something down a hole!"

"Thank goodness for excited dogs." His father chuckled.

"Will Tom agree, do you think," Eduard asked his half-brother.

"There's a risk, of course, Eduard. But you know Tom almost as well as do I. He'll agree. And do it spang right on, I guarantee."

"I think so, too. If Plume is an example of the Very Worst, Tom is among the Very Best of Men! So, so be it! I'll send Arcolas in, shall I?"

Courtroom spectators stood, suddenly quiet, as King Eduard Tenth Trusslo entered and took his place at the plain wooden desk that served him as his Bench.

"Bring the prisoner in," he ordered the Clerk. Clerk nodded and spoke to the Chief Bailiff who trotted to the side door to his right.

"Prisoner will stand to hear the Court's verdict," Clerk said, more than a bit nervously.

Plume was even more nervous, shaking like an aspen leaf, panting—but silent.

"Prisoner has been found guilty as charged on all counts," Eduard announced.

Bailiffs stepped forward to catch the sagging Plume.

Clerk slowly and carefully read the list of charges, pausing and then adding the word "Guilty" after each.

A tremulous sigh or sob or relieved murmur rustled through the huge ballroom and far beyond.

Furbetrance blew a sad ring of grey smoke from his nostrils, trying to look regretful.

Tom embraced Manda and Gay. Manda tried very hard to look severe, but failed. Gay was obviously stunned and clutched her father's left hand very tightly.

Murdan stood and addressed the Court.

"Is the Royal Court ready to impose sentence, Lord?"

"Yes. Even in such a case, it's very difficult to do—but must be done, as best a King can.

"Convict Plume, I impose the least objectionable of the proscribed, possible sentences.

"I hereby sentence you, Convict Plume of Overall, to perpetual banishment from the Kingdom of Carolna. If you ever return here you will be punished by instant and complete death.

"So sayeth I, Eduard Tenth Trusslo, King and Chief Justice of Carolna. And may the Good God have mercy on your soul!"

"Take Convict Plume to his place of banishment, Sir Thomas!"

Tom bowed slightly and clapped his hands together sharply.

Librarian and Convict...*disappeared.*

"We'll wait here, then?" Manda asked.

"You understand the sentence, then?" Queen Beatrix asked, dabbing the tears from her cheeks.

"Oh, I have no quarrel with the sentence or having Tom carry it out," the Princess said with a bit of quaver. "Look! It's raining hard again..."

A tremendous roar of thunder and flash of lightning drowned her words. A great push of cold wind swept down the valley from the Snow Mountains and battered at the three tall towers of Overhall.

A curtain of black rain was drawn across the land. Manda and Gay and Brenda, the King, and Queen Beatrix, many friends and servants, three enormous Dragons—and the dog Blackly—stood on the empty ballroom...and waited.

A raw wind swept across the wide lawn and rain obscured the white dome of a tall, dignified building.

"*Damn!* How'd you do that?" Plume swore. "Where *are* we?"

"You don't recognize the Capitol?" Tom asked. "This is Washington and it's late spring and if you wait a day or two, it'll warm up."

"Y-y-you brought me back to this place! I thought…"

"They say the summers are getting warmer and the winters colder," Tom told him. "It's called something like *Global Warming*, I think. Or was it *Nuclear Winter?*"

A strong gust of wet wind caught at their sleeves and blasted their faces with fine mist.

"Washington! Back in our old USA! I would rather be almost anywhere else. Must still be some nice, warm, lovely ice floes in the sea, isn't there? You must know the right spellings! Take me back! I'll reform. I promise I'll change! Anywhere but here and now, Tom! Sir Thomas, I mean. I *beg* you!"

His pitch rose with the wind until he fairly shrieked.

Tom shook his head. "There are a lot of nice, warm places where you could shelter, Plume. Over there is the National Archives. You could warm up in the Modern Art Gallery. I hear there are even people who will feed you hot soup and bread. Ask that policeman, over there."

"*Policeman!* Where?"

A cloud of fine, grey mist swirled about them.

"Well…" the Librarian began.

"What will your lovely, merciful Princess Manda say? Leave me here! *She* would have mercy! Such a nice, sweet girl, your Manda."

"Plume! Calm yourself. Behave yourself—but if you can't—be very careful!"

Tom struck his palms together three times, firmly.

The Metropolitan Police officer strode up to the shivering felon.

"Need some help, sir?" He clutched Plume's left elbow as the little man began to crumble. "Here, sit down on the bench, sir. I'll get some help for you."

"Tom! Sir Thomas, I mean!"

But on the Mall just then there were only a uniformed policeman, a quaking convict—and a flock of curious, grey-and-white pigeons.

"Won't he figure out how to come back to Carolna, even so?" Manda asked, her head resting on her husband's shoulder. "Plume was always really smart about such things."

"Possible, but not very likely. He'd have to have somebody at *this* end of the—well, I guess—the universe. To bring him back. Only you and I and Arcolas have any idea where he's been hidden, dear Princess-love. And we have sense enough to be silent."

"But, won't Plume starve to death? I mean, what *could* he do to earn food and shelter?"

"A trained Accountant can always find work. For that matter, a crooked Accountant probably would do even better in the States, these days. For a while, anyway."

Manda sat up straight and sniffed at a breeze coming from the castle bakery, far below.

"You're right, as usual, Papa. Personally, I would've..."

Tom waited a long moment, then asked, "You would've done what?"

"I would've happily sprung the trap on the gallows when my father the King had him hung. Or *hanged*. Whichever is right."

She sniffed appreciatively. "Apple pie! Let's go beg a slice or two off Murdan's Master Baker, Tom! I haven't craved apple pie since—whenever!"

The Historian had followed the practice of his many worthy predecessors in establishing a special Scribe to copy, compound and clarify a *Greater History of the Kingdom of Carolna*.

He now leaned forward in his high-backed chair and scowled at his Scribe, who sat opposite him across the highly polished desk.

"You want to quit? *Quit!* You've only been here for—what?"

"Forty three years, seven months, three days and two hours, Lord Historian. I promise to finish my *Current Events* notes, up to the trial of the Accountant, but when things become quiet, I want to slip away, do a little traveling, maybe some surf casting. Visit my four children, six grandchildren, and two great-grandchildren."

"I wish being a Royal Historian had such an easy end," Murdan sighed. "Granted! But be sure to finish *Current Events* before you leave."

The History Scribe bowed, vowed his gratitude, and slid off to his own quiet corner of the Library where an assistant brought him a cup of tea.

The Librarian, who had listened to the exchange from his own desk, chuckled.

"You are so wickedly devious!"

"Me? *Devious!* I was but rewarding a faithful servant who is grown old…"

"*Very* old. And when do you think *Current Events* will be finished?"

"Well, 'current' means to go on forever."

"Devious, as I said. And I do hope you will want to keep me at least as long."

"Small hope of that! There's the matter of your disposition of a certain number-cruncher. Where is he?"

"Perhaps when I'm as old and worn out as yonder Scribe, I'll tell you. Perhaps."

Murdan hid a smile behind his scowl and shrugged.

You told Manda, I know. And Arcolas told me. Still, Plume's secret is well-kept, I'm positive!

But he didn't say the words aloud.

"A question, however," Tom said. "It is spring and the apple trees are in full bloom. Where did Baker get apples for pies?"

"Some things are best kept secret—for the good of Elfkind and Mankind, my boy."

On sharp-edged Obsidian Cliffs overlooking the flood-brown waters of the mighty Cristol River, Retruance, his brother Furbetrance, and the young Brazier, relaxed in the afternoon sun,

"You did a difficult job very well, I think, Daddy," the boy assured his father.

"I will second that motion," Retruance rumbled without opening his eyes.

"I really didn't do as well as I'd hoped—or planned." Furbie shrugged—a movement akin to a small earthquake that shook loose bits of black volcanic glass into the river far below.

"No regrets, however. We Constables are proud of you both. You may *take that to the bank,* as Tom says. Whatever a bank is."

Furbetrance groaned. "Well, maybe now we'll have time for some field training, Son."

Brazier rolled over on his back to let the sun warm his tummy and chest.

"There's no hurry, is there?" he asked. "We only just stopped working and running and such exciting things."

His uncle grunted and gently prodded him in the tummy with his sharp-pointed tail.

"You have yet to learn," said he, "that 'things' never stop happening. They just slow down a bit, now and then."

Brazier, lifting the tip of his right wing to shade his eyes from the sun, quickly changed the subject. "There's a ship in the mouth of the bay. Strange looking rig; all raggedy. I wonder from whence it hails."

ABOUT THE AUTHOR

Donald Bruce Callander
1930 -- July 25, 2008

Don Callander was the best-selling author of the 'Mancer series and the Dragon Companion series. Don originally worked as a travel writer/ photographer and graphic designer before retiring to start his writing.

Don was born in Minneapolis, brought up in Duluth, Minnesota, and graduated from high school there before enlisting in the U. S. Navy in 1947. After serving four years on active duty (including the Korean War) he transferred to the Naval Reserve where he served as a 'weekend warrior' for twenty additional years.

He settled in Washington, D.C., where he married, raised four children, and worked on the Washington Post newspaper and in National Headquarters of the American Automobile Association (40,000,000 members!) until his retirement in 1991.

CPSIA information can be obtained at www.ICGtesting.com
Printed in the USA
LVOW12s1154191214

419399LV00002B/410/P